By Angela Kay Austin

Beale Street Blues
Rumer
Give Me Everything
Derailed
Sweet Victory
Scarlet's Tears
Love All over Me

Coming Soon

Love's Chance
Freedom

Beale Street Blues

Angela Kay Austin

Copyright © 2014 Bluff City Publishing, L.L.C.

Edited by Leanore Elliott

Cover Art by Fiona Jayde Media

EBook ISBN: 978-0-9863137-1-4

ISBN-13: 978-0-9863137-2-1

For information, address: Bluff City Publishing, L.L.C., P.O. Box 300934, Memphis, TN 38130

DEDICATION

Does starting over mean you've lost? No. It means
you've been given the chance for a new chapter. This
book is dedicated to everyone who's not afraid to pack the
trunk of their car and give it one more try.

ACKNOWLEDGMENTS

This one is for my parents. Without whom I would not have been able to start over again, and again and again.

PROLOGUE

The twists and turns of the streets of downtown Memphis drained what little energy Darling Crawford had remaining. She wasn't twenty-one anymore and didn't have the desire or money to party all night long. But, what were her options? Sit at home with her parents and waste another Friday night.

Finally!

Before the truck could pull out of its parking spot, she'd begun to swing her car across traffic to the other side of the road. *Screw the angry horns, honking; I have out of state tags.* If she didn't get this one, she'd have to cough up fifteen dollars to park. And that wasn't going to happen.

Darling parked and then grabbed her clutch bag from the backseat. With her purse gripped underneath her arm, she strolled down Union. The stories her grandfather and parents told her of the old days and Beale Street flooded her mind as she strolled through the historic neighborhood. Muddy Waters, Memphis Minnie, Louis Armstrong, and B.B. King had all played at the clubs on

Beale back in the day. Beale had been through a few transitions since then. When Darling was a child, many of the shops on Beale were closed and boarded up. But now, the streets were lined with trendy shops, restaurants, and clubs.

AutoZone Park, Memphis' minor league baseball team's stadium, loomed out of the darkness at her. Neon baseballs and bats affixed to its façade lit her path. As she neared Peabody Place, a late addition to the famed Peabody Hotel, she glanced through the plate glass windows at the Memphis elite. Women dripping in sparkly jewels laughed as they chatted with men dressed in expensive suits, instead of boys wearing jeans.

Thirteen dollars minimum for a glass of wine! Not her idea of a cheap night.

She kept walking.

Darling shifted her weight from one foot to the other as she stood waiting on the octogenarian, waving the wand along the length of the back of the young black man in front of her. When it was her turn, she flashed her I.D. and gritted her teeth in an attempt to hold onto the ounce of patience she had left. It never went smoothly and this time was no different.

The woman asked her to step through the gate and to the side. A younger female security guard asked her to open her bag, after glancing through it, she asked Darling to stretch out her arms. The woman slid her hands along the length of Darling's waist smoothing the cotton of her red dress as she did. Then, she bent and ran her hands along the black boots she wore.

As the woman finished, Darling turned her attention to the sadness of the harmonica that spilled out of the bar onto Beale Street beckoning to her as it had done so often over the past months. The slow slide of the guitar accompanying the harmonica's wordless pain and sorrow spoke to her broken heart. What could be more appropriate, she thought as she paid her three dollars—

she'd forgotten it wasn't free on Fridays. She'd rather join the Elvis junkies, drunken conference attendees, starlet wannabes and lost souls with nowhere to be and no one to be with than strangers in a dark room sipping cheap liquor while they ate saucy spicy barbeque.

Seated in her normal spot, Darling squeezed her eyes shut to close out the corny flirtations of the velvet-clad singer, and let the sad lyrics of the down-home Delta blues slink across her body and mind. The singer longed for the return of his lover, as she'd wished so many nights for hers. It was stupid, she knew it. He'd abandoned her.

The beat of the music dragged her body with it. Slowly, her feet tapped and her shoulders swayed. As the singer sang to his mystery lover, she remembered the touch of her own. His mouth against hers. The sensation of his hands to her breasts. The feel of his fingers as he dragged them along the length of her legs.

How could I still want someone who didn't want a damn thing to do with me?

She stepped onto the dance floor and allowed the vocalist to sing only to her. Her body followed the baseline of the music. She didn't care what the people watching her thought.

Her eyes sprang open at the feel of a hand on her arm. Eyes the color of the deepest emeralds asked her permission, wordlessly. She placed her hand on his waist allowing him to pull her closer. A mixture of mandarin and persimmon filled her senses as he tightened his hold. One hand rested on the small of her back, while the other lay on her hip, guiding her to his rhythm.

Too much time had passed since she'd felt the warmth and strength of a man, especially a man like this one. She glanced up to find him watching.

His eyes locked on hers and he smiled.

The confidence in his smile and the warmth of his touch sparked a flame inside her. She couldn't resist reaching up to rake her fingers through the salt and pepper curls at his temple.

He closed his eyes at the touch of her hand. When he opened them, his gaze was too intense to hold.

She allowed herself to be lost in the fantasy of the man and the music. But when the music ended, regretfully, they would go to their separate corners.

"Excuse me," he spoke in a deep male voice with a definite southern accent.

Damn! His voice rippled through her mind and across her skin, taking over where the dance with her stranger had ended. She opened her eyes to find herself staring into the green eyes of one of the most beautiful men she'd ever seen.

The gentle smile he wore touched the corners of his eyes tugging them down slightly. "Hi. Am I disturbing you?"

There it was again…his southern drawl made her want to keep listening to whatever he said next. *Yes, you are disturbing me but…don't stop talking.* "No."

"I didn't introduce myself earlier." He extended a hand. "Jaxon."

The strength of his hand was matched by its warmth. The simple touch made her want to pull away and hold on at the same time. He belonged at the Peabody with the women adorned in diamonds, not here with her. "Darling."

He raised an eyebrow at the mention of her name. "Darling. Interesting name." He tempted her with the sound of her name as his eyes took in all of her.

"Thank my grandmother." She smiled. "I'm lucky it wasn't Sugar or Belle."

"Or a mix of the two." He laughed. "I think they definitely made the right choice." He sipped from his glass. "You love music?"

With her glass, she pointed at the singer and his band on stage. "This is one of the best bands I've found in Memphis."

Jaxon nodded, leaning a little closer. "I come here whenever I'm in Memphis." He flashed a heartbreaking smile that formed those little parentheses along his cheeks.

She leaned a little closer because she wanted to. "Often?" It didn't matter, but she was curious.

"Regularly...for work." He looked at her empty glass. "Can I get you a refill?"

She couldn't keep dipping into her 401K money. He could buy anything he wanted. "Dirty martini," she said, "Thanks." It wouldn't get him anywhere. Maybe another dance, but that's all. If she were a few years younger, maybe she could play the game of one night stand. But, she wasn't trying to be bought with a few drinks and a dance. And that was all she really had to offer him or anybody else.

An hour later, his easy manner and casual conversation combined with drinks that had been endless since his arrival kept her talking and dancing much longer than she'd originally intended, beating down her desire to leave without him.

So much about this man reminded her of the one who'd left her.

"Where are you from?" he asked, the warmth of his breath breezed across her ear, as he leaned closer in an attempt to compete with the music of the live blues band.

Was it the martinis or did his cologne wrap around her, and pull her in with no hope of her escaping him? Why did she want to? How long had it been since she'd been close to a man that she wanted? She crossed and uncrossed her legs to calm her mind, but it only excited her body more. "Here."

Jaxon quirked an eyebrow. "Yeah? Where's your Memphis accent?"

"Never had one." She grabbed the toothpick, spearing the olives in her glass and slid one off. Popping it into her mouth, she closed her eyes and savored the blend of the olive and her vodka. When she opened her eyes, his green gaze stared at her mouth as if he wanted a taste, too. But, not of the olives. And she truly wanted to allow him.

Something in his gaze changed. He reached out and wrapped an arm around her waist. "Let me show you Memphis."

Did she really want to leave with him? Could she trust this man? He could be an axe murderer.

Slowly, his hand moved up and down the length of her back. "Trust me." He smiled. "You'll love it."

"Okay." Why not? She stood, and he waved down the bartender. Outside of the front entrance, a crush of bodies briefly slowed her exit and he caught up to her.

With a touch of his hand to her elbow, he guided her through the crowd of drunks and underage teenagers who couldn't enter the clubs along Beale. It was early by Beale Street time, and the crowd created its own party in the streets. The horde waited for whatever opportunity presenting itself as inebriated club hoppers came and went.

"Where are we going?" she asked. *Back to his hotel?*

At the corner of Beale and Second, he flagged down a carriage. Adorned in orange and white lights, maybe in preparation for Halloween, the Cinderella inspired buggy pulled up in front of them. He winked at her as he assisted her into the back of the carriage. He spread a blanket which had been neatly folded in a corner across her lap and draped his arm across her shoulders.

The fitted sweater dress she wore was all she really needed on an October night in Memphis. But, she snuggled a little closer against his solid chest and pulled the blanket higher on her lap.

"Downtown Memphis is beautiful at night," he said. "Nashville is where I spend most of my time. It's beautiful, too, but there's something about Memphis." He rubbed his chin against the top of her head.

"I just moved here from Charlotte," she admitted. "I get lost every time I hop into my car, especially down here with all the one way streets." She laughed. "You don't want to know how many times I've crossed the bridge into Arkansas and had to loop back around."

"You don't have a GPS?" he asked while he rubbed his hand up and down her right shoulder.

Darling snuggled a little closer and let the madness of the night take over. "I have an app on my phone, but I don't really go out that often. I never really think to use it."

She listened as he shared his love for Memphis with her. The carriage driver drove by historic landmarks pointing out things she didn't know about her own hometown.

When they pulled up to one of the old bars she'd hung out at before, he asked the driver to stop. "Have you been to this place before?" he asked.

"Sure." They had a monthly free wine event. She'd been a few times. "But, not recently. Why?"

A slow sexy grin spread across his face. "Did you know it's famous because back in the old days, it used to be a brothel?"

No, she didn't. Was he hinting at something, finally making his move? "No."

"They're also famous for their burgers." He winked again. "Are you hungry?"

She'd been having such a great time, she hadn't thought about eating. Now, that he'd mentioned it. Her stomach responded.

He paid the driver, and helped her out of the carriage.

Inside the restaurant, she sipped at another martini while they waited on burgers and fries. "So, why'd you bring me here? Is this your way of hinting at what you want?"

"Hinting." He reached over and rubbed his hand along her thigh. "I'm a more direct guy." Jaxon pulled his hand away and combed his fingers through her hair. "If you have a question, you should ask me."

What was she thinking? This man was too damn beautiful. Her ex was beautiful, too. A beautiful cheat and liar who had no problem spreading that *beauty* around. This one was probably no different. But, he wasn't her husband and she expected nothing from him at all. She smiled right back at him. "Who are you Jaxon?"

"That's all you want to know?" he asked.

"For now." She bit into the burger the waitress sat in front of her.

"I'm in town for business." He bit into his own burger. After he swallowed, he continued, "My family's business allows me to travel a lot." He stared at her for a moment, and then said, "I'm not married, if that's what you're asking."

"No, I wasn't asking." But, it was good to know. She had no plans to be similar in any way to the woman who ripped her home apart.

He wiggled the knot of his tie, loosening it. "Sorry, I thought you might be curious."

She was right this guy was so out of her league. *His family's business.* Maybe he could give her a job. On second thought working for a man like him wouldn't be a good idea. She'd never think about anything, but getting him into bed. "You like your business?"

"It gives me what I need." He drank from his beer, allowing his eyes to roam her body as he leaned back in his chair. "And what about you Miss Darling?"

"Me?" *Separated. Broke.* "Moved here from Charlotte. Not sure what's next, yet." And she didn't want to talk about it anymore. "Where are you staying tonight?"

"Are you asking out of curiosity?" he asked.

"Is it far?"

Jaxon leaned near and whispered against her ear, "I'll give you one chance to change your mind." He pulled back and locked his gaze on hers. He waved over the waitress and paid the tab. "I'm staying at the Peabody."

From the suit he wore, she knew he had money and his choice of hotel confirmed it. There wasn't much more *traditional* Memphis than The Peabody, Beale Street, and the freaking Mississippi river. All of which he'd shown her tonight. He must be *old* south. Old Memphis. Full of tradition and expectations.

###

When Jaxon closed the door of his hotel room behind them, emboldened by the liquor raging through her blood, Darling released the pent up passion she felt for her southern gentleman stranger. The first man in a long time that made her want to be where she was and about to do what she was about to do.

She pressed him into the door behind him and touched her lips to his. The softness of his lips against hers increased a hunger inside of her that she'd either forgotten or satiated with liquor and her own talented fingers. But, tonight those fingers slid through his hair pulling his head down to her and still, she needed to crane her neck and stand on her tiptoes to reach him.

Thick arms tightened around her waist, lifting her from the floor. One hand held her tight to his body, the other traveled down her back to her butt. "Wrap your legs around my waist," he commanded with that damn southern drawl.

Darling readily obeyed.

Her butt rested in his hands. Slowly, he lifted her body, and then let it fall, repeatedly. With each motion she could feel the firmness and fullness of him grow—it fed her hunger for him. She reached between them and wrapped her hand around the bulge pressing against her most sensitive skin. He moaned in response to her touch. Hot and thick in her hand, she ached to feel him inside her. Maybe he could help her forget everything. "Where is your bedroom?"

He motioned to a room on the right.

She dropped her feet to the floor and dragged him through the suite behind her, now almost desperate with need. Red and blue lights from Beale Street below cut through the darkness of the bedroom. Darling used the weird glow to lead him to the edge of his bed and pushed him onto it.

Jaxon stripped his suit jacket off and she helped with his shirt. His shoulders were broad—not bodybuilder crazy—but defined. With her fingers, she traced the reflection of the red and blue lights that streaked across his chest. The feel of his warm skin beneath her fingertips further intensified the desire building within her to know everything about him. The need—for him—became more urgent the longer she touched him.

He stripped his pants away and dropped them on the floor...Waiting.

Her eyes crawled over his body, but she couldn't decide whether to focus her gaze on him or watch his hand as he massaged his swelling cock. The sleeves of the dress she wore slipped from her shoulders, the fabric sliding down to pool at her feet. She stood in front of him with only her thong separating them. "Condoms?"

He grabbed his pants and pulled his wallet from one of the pockets. When he was too slow rolling it on, she reached out, impatiently, to help. Crouching to her knees, she rotated between using her hands to push the latex down the length of him, and her mouth to tease. His body arched and thrust forward before she pulled away to kiss the tanned skin of his stomach.

One powerful arm reached out and pulled her to her full height. "Come here." With a finger he hooked her panties and pulled them from her body before laying her across his bed.

The weight of his body on top of hers warmed her, not from the cold, but something inside of her began to wake. It'd been a long time since she'd felt the touch of a man and she ached for so much more than just a touch from this man. His fingers worked her body until the only thing that would satisfy her was him. He moved his hand and flipped them both over, so that she was on top of him and he rested against the headboard. She lowered herself onto him, slowly. For a moment, he waited for her to move again. But then, he grabbed her hips, and pulled her tight to his body.

Jaxon's head fell back to the headboard, his eyes closed, as he thrust himself deeper inside her. The thickness of him filled her and she moaned with pleasure

His eyes opened.

One hand reached toward her face, but she grabbed it and his other one and pinned them to the bed while she slowly grinded her body against his. The upward movement of his hips increased with his moans.

The feel of his hot damp skin, his moans and the energy building inside of her…excited her. She wanted more and more and she took it. She threw her head back and arched her back, enjoying every moment of her ride and every inch of her southern gentleman.

The muscles of his arms and stomach tightened. She stared into his eyes as she jockeyed back and forth. The intensity of his gaze, a mixture of pleasure along with hunger claimed her, and she didn't want to see it fade. Harder and harder she moved.

He bit his bottom lip as he matched his thrusts to hers. Tanned pecs flexed and he groaned, "Darling."

Her name from his mouth sparked a flame buried deep within her; she flexed her hips while eliciting one last moan from him and herself. The nerves of her body tingled from her toes to her nipples.

As the ripples of her orgasm seized, all she could think about was jumping on top of him again. But, with the stillness of her body, came sanity. Months had passed since she'd had sex. No matter how many men she'd given her number to since moving to Memphis, she never bothered to return any of their calls. What would she do when they came to pick her up for their date? Sure, she could meet them for a while and go to their place, but eventually, they'd want to come to her home or spend the night. That wasn't going to happen anytime soon. So, if she couldn't go on a date, that meant she definitely couldn't take any of them up on their offers or promises of being the *best* she'd ever had. She didn't think anyone could make that promise again, because the man beside her now had that honor.

Her ex always needed a little assistance from her favorite vibrator to get her to where this man got her with just a touch and a kiss. She slammed her eyes closed, and tried to will her senses back to normal. What was she doing? No matter how lonely she'd been, picking up a strange man on Beale Street wasn't going to fix any of her problems. She rose from the bed, and inside of minutes, she'd gathered her clothing and dressed, then sprinted toward Jaxon's hotel door.

"Wait." He trailed behind her, naked. "Can I see you again?"

She stood with her hand on his hotel door. They never should've had sex and it definitely wouldn't happen again. What did she have to offer *him*? She stared at the naked man in the middle of the room. She didn't want to, but couldn't resist another opportunity to commit Jaxon to memory. Damn, expensive clothes or a paper bag, he would look gorgeous. Although, they'd just left his bed, the thickness and length of his rod didn't seem to know that. "What for?"

Jaxon took a step back as he stared over at the bedroom they'd just left. "I don't know—dinner." He snatched a pad from the nearby desk and scribbled something on it, then handed it to her.

His number. "Maybe."

The whole night had been a huge mistake. Fun—but a mistake. Her body quivered at the freaking thought of what he'd just done to it. There was too much she had to do and screwing around with some rich guy who wouldn't know where the poor neighborhoods of South Memphis was if she circled it on a map, wasn't going to help her any.

Darling tossed the piece of paper into the trash before she stepped onto the elevator. She didn't need anything to remind her of how pathetic she'd become.

CHAPTER ONE

*D*amn. Darling sprang up from her sleep, instantly awake and annoyed. The train rumbling over the tracks nearby rattled her bedroom windows as it passed. Why did the engineer drag out the loud horn? Weren't the lights and big freaking automatic arms enough? As the horn faded into the distance, she snuggled back under the covers her mother had layered onto her bed. It wouldn't matter, but maybe, this time, she'd be able to fall back to sleep. Every night it was the same thing. How was she supposed to be prepared for the next day, when she could never get enough sleep?

Her eyes were open long before the chime of her cell phone sang at her. She heaved one leg after the other and dragged herself out of bed toward the bathroom. The closed door and scent of cigarette smoke told her it was occupied. *Dad.* She turned around and headed back to her bedroom. *Three grown people. One bathroom!*

Her head fell into her hands. Tears filled the palms of her hands. The plan had been to move back in with her parents until she could get things back together. But, she'd been living with them for four months now, because she wasn't making enough money to cover her debts. She also fought every day with her ex over the divorce. The longer he dragged it out, the more her accounts dwindled. Leaving Charlotte had made sense when she did it, but now, it just seemed plain dumb.

Stupid! Why did she quit her job and walk away from everything?

"It's all yours," her father yelled.

###

Starbucks thermos in hand, filled with coffee from home, Darling sped around 240 east. Driving from South Memphis to Bartlett—forty-five minutes—everyday was not exactly fun, but a job was a job. She swung her car into the first spot she saw, prepped for a quick sec, and then strolled into the offices of Slater Enterprises.

She pasted one of her biggest smiles on her face, waved and nodded at everyone she passed in the halls on the way to her office. She'd almost made it when one of her Customer Service Reps caught her.

"Excuse me, Ms. Darling, but has my leave request been approved?"

"Sam, I'm sorry it took so long, but yes...yes of course, there should be no problem. I'll email you the official approval today."

"Thank you." With that, Sam disappeared back into the call center.

Darling sank into her office chair, and scanned the beige room with its beige computer and brown furniture. God, was this really going to be her new life?

###

Remote control in hand, Darling stretched out on the

couch in her parents' den. Wine and television had become her two closest friends. *How sad.* But, what else was there to do in Memphis? Especially, when you had absolutely no money in the bank to do it with.

"Darling, what're ya gonna cook?" her father asked.

Traditional to a fault. Her father expected women to cook, iron his clothes and if she were to be honest, not ask too many questions of the man. But, he also respected his woman, her mother and would never do anything to betray her, his home or his children. He could definitely teach her ex a few things. As 1950's as it was, she would love to find a man that believed in traditions as long as it didn't mean she'd have to wear a set of pearl handcuffs. "Cook? Nothing. I ate a bowl of cereal."

"Cereal." Her father turned and walked back toward the kitchen. "I guess I'll fry some pork steak for ya mama and me. She'll be hungry when she gets back from church."

That was her pop. He could cook, but he didn't because he thought it was a woman's role. "Sounds good, pop." She kept flipping through the channels.

He paused and stared at her for a minute longer than necessary. "Sure you don't want some."

"Positive. Thanks pop." All she really wanted, selfishly, was a little privacy.

While her father banged around pots and pans, she focused, or tried to focus on the images on the screen as they began to blur. She gave up and let the hazy pictures lull her off to sleep.

If felt as if hours had passed, when Darling woke and pressed the menu button on the remote control. According to the time displayed, she'd only been asleep for about twenty minutes. She went back to flipping channels. The channel for women. Love stories. She pressed the info button. What? Two people meet on an elevator and find true love. Oh, God, please. She'd met her *almost* ex-husband through a friend, and they'd dated for three years before they married. As clichéd as it sounds, the seven year itch exists. Nothing she tried, saved her marriage.

Love at first sight was make believe.

The more she thought of her ex, the angrier she became, and the dumber the show on television seemed. She rose from the couch, clicked the TV off and stomped toward *her* bedroom passing the computer room that had once been another bedroom like hers, only much pinker with yellow stars on every wall. She stared at her hands as she remembered the way she and Charity spent more time painting each other than the walls. Her mother had to throw them both into the tub and scrub them within an inch of their lives to remove all the paint. She shut the door to the room and kept walking.

She stood in the middle of her bedroom which seemed so big when she was a child, staring. The room barely seemed large enough for the full sized bed centered below a window on a far wall. She walked to the door and closed it, leaning her back against it.

Why?

There wasn't space to breathe or think. She paced back and forth, stubbing her toe on a box of clothes she'd tucked into a corner because there was no closet to put them in. Damn it! She flung the wine glass she held at the furthest wall. The glass splintered into tiny shards of light. The chocolate scent of the red wine perfumed the room as the liquid left an ominous trail on the wall.

The door to her bedroom flung open banging against the wall to demand her attention. She looked to find her parents' concerned eyes glued to her. "What's wrong?" they asked.

One look at the wall and her father whispered something to her mother, then turned and walked away. But her mother, still dressed in her Sunday best because she'd just come from bible study, walked right in with her bible in hand and sat on the bed.

Darling sat beside her unable to look into her eyes.

Instead, she watched the wine drizzle down the wall to the carpeted floor beneath. She would have to paint the wall and shampoo that carpet before the stain became permanent.

Her mother wrapped her arms around her. "I know you don't think we can understand what you're going through, but maybe we can still help."

The comfort of her mother's arms calmed the angry voice inside of her head.

"Baby, tell me what's wrong?" Her mother asked in an unsteady voice.

Really? Cry on her mother's shoulder? Was this it? Once again living in the room, she slept in as a child discussing her problems with her mother.

This has to be a crazy dream.

She pinched herself as she pulled away from her mother's embrace.

Wake up! Wake up, now!

It was painfully obvious her mother wasn't leaving and she had no way to escape. She leaned against the cold wall that butted up against the bed in place of a headboard. "Mom, how did this happen?" She rubbed the fingers of one hand against her temple at the stinging that throbbed angrily.

"What?" Her mother's blank expression supported her question.

"Me…this…" Darling gestured with one hand at the room. "I should be helping you, not living off you."

"You're not living off us. We've wanted you back home for so long."

"Mom, why did I allow this to happen? I can't stop the divorce, but quitting my job. Stupid!" She paused. "I just wanted to get away from everything."

"I wish that I had the answers you need," she responded. "My Darling, some people don't treasure marriage for what it is." Her mom glanced toward her own bedroom. "Your father and I didn't have an easy marriage, but we loved each other and we fought for it. Hard." She reached for Darling's hand and squeezed it softly. "Steve wasn't the right man for you. But, I'm confident your special someone is still looking for you."

"Oh, mom, you're such a hopeless romantic." She closed her eyes and for a moment, allowed images of Jaxon, the gorgeous stranger from Beale Street to flash through her mind. "I wish I believed in romance and love like you do."

"When you met Steve, I think you were ready to love because for so long, you wouldn't." Her mother paused. "When we lost your sister...I don't think we knew how much that affected you until you were older." Her mother's head bowed. "We should've known. We should've done more."

They'd been young, but no matter how young you are, you shouldn't be playing kick ball with your baby sister one minute and the next, the ball rolls into the street, the brakes of a car screech...and your sister's gone. She rubbed the spot on her leg where the scar blazed that constantly reminded her of how she was too weak to drag her sister out of the street.

Tears welled, but they didn't fall as she remembered her mother as she'd seen her all those years ago sitting in almost the exact spot trying to explain Charity's death. Instead, she'd spent hours comforting her mother as an endless stream of tears soaked them both.

"You were always so strong." Her mother's hand slid along her chin. "But maybe, now it's time for you to let someone else help you. That could be why you're here."

She stared at the stain on the wall. "Mom, I really thought he loved me."

"I know." Her mom kissed her on the forehead and stood to walk away. "Maybe it's time for you to love yourself. Maybe because we've missed you and we need you as much as you need us. Whatever the reason, we're all together. Family should be together."

21

Family should be together.

Fully clothed, Darling climbed underneath the covers. Sleep…that was all she needed. Everything would look better tomorrow. No matter how long she laid there, nothing happened. Until…images of her beautiful green eyed Jaxon filled her mind and warmed her from the inside out. She allowed the images of him to take over. Again, the scent of persimmon flooded her senses. The confidence and strength of his hold around her waist sent shivers down her spine. Jaxon had made love to her like she was the only one he'd wanted. Tonight, she would give anything to be in his arms again. If she could feel his lips against hers, one more time all the other crap might be worth it.

CHAPTER TWO

Mornings sucked. And the worst thing about this one was that it was Friday morning. Darling should be happy like normal hard-working people, but Friday morning meant that she wouldn't hear back from any of the recruiters she'd reached out to until Monday, if she didn't hear today. *If I heard anything at all.*

At least she wouldn't have to think about anything over the weekend. She could sleep all day Saturday and Sunday. No plans whatsoever.

Again, she dragged herself through the day. Periodically, she stared at the clock as if she wanted to beat it with a bat if it didn't continue to do its job. And today, would be even longer because she had to go to lunch with co-workers, including her boss, who, she felt sure, believed she would eventually end up in his bed. Apparently, his wife didn't know she shared him with several of the women in the office.

Sucks!

A few hours later, everyone huddled around a table in a

private area of the cafeteria, waiting on their boss to grace them with his appearance. The desire to bang her fists against the table and scream overwhelmed her. She swallowed a laugh, but eagle-eyed Barbara, superstar meeting guru, still noticed.

Just as she figured out what lie would be an acceptable excuse to leave, Rodney Burch popped in. Darling heard the faint ding of a microwave in the background and the delicious smell of buttery popcorn wafted through the door behind Rodney.

"Team, sorry that I'm late." He paused to look over his shoulder. "I have a huge surprise." Again, he glanced over his shoulder. This time he turned around with one of his classic big crap grins on his face. "The owner of our wonderful company, Slater Enterprises, Jaxon Slater, flew in to join us for our luncheon to welcome our new team member, Darling."

Jaxon? Couldn't be!

A man with too familiar a face stepped from the background to join Rodney. She would recognize the way Jaxon moved no matter where they were or when. As he walked up to join Rodney, flashes of him moving around the dance floor with her in his arms hit her hard. She swore she could feel his arms holding her, his hands resting on the small of her back guiding her to exactly where he wanted her next.

The man's physique dwarfed Rodney and emphasized Rodney's need to join a gym, immediately. Beautiful green eyes met hers briefly before focusing on Rodney.

Darling tried to shake off the feeling that she thought she saw anger in his eyes.

"I'd like to introduce all of you to Jaxon Slater," Rodney said.

The guru jumped from her seat with her hand extended and approached Jaxon. "Nice to meet you again, sir."

Could she kiss his butt any more than she kissed Rodney's? Rumor had it, she did a lot more than that and from the way she kept licking her lips at Jaxon Slater, she had plans there, too.

Slut!

"Sir," Rodney interrupted, "you remember Barbara Kearns. She helped us with a lot of our meeting planning last year."

"Yes, of course, Barbara, a pleasure to see you again." He smiled.

Crap! Darling sipped from the glass of iced tea in front of her, but it didn't cool her off. No matter how much time had passed, she couldn't forget that voice. The touch of his lips against her skin and the soft mumble of her name against her stomach along with one too many vodka martinis created a night—the only passion filled night she'd had in Memphis—she hadn't been able to forget.

He walked around the table greeting everyone until he reached her.

"Mr. Slater, this is our newest team member, Darling Crawford. She's done a great job for us. Fitting right in with the team," Rodney said. "I thought she might be the best person to assist us with the meeting calendar this year."

"What?" Barbara asked. She pinned Rodney to the wall with her stare.

"Darling." Jaxon smiled. "That is a unique name. Hard to forget." He extended his hand. "Nice to meet you."

"Thank you, sir." How did she end up in this position? Nothing good ever comes from a one-night stand. *Well, almost nothing.* Her one night with Jaxon had given her something she hadn't had in a long time. A night of romance.

"Please." He glanced around the table. "Everyone call me Jaxon." He pulled out the chair beside Darling. "Is anyone sitting here?"

"No," Rodney answered for her.

An intoxicating scent of persimmon overtook her as he sat beside her. Her dress, her hair, her skin it all smelled of persimmon and amber when she'd left him that night. It'd been too damn hard to wash the scent from the dress the next day. Distance was what she needed. Immediately. She slid her chair away from his. *Just a little.*

"Sir," Kathy addressed him, "How long will you be in town?"

He glanced around the table. "I'm not sure, yet. But, I thought I'd meet with a few of you while I was here. Get an idea of how you feel the company is doing and how we're treating you. Memphis is one of our key markets. Everything at this office is extremely important to me."

Stripping, as he walked through his hotel room, Jaxon tossed his suit jacket across the bed, ignoring it when it slid to the floor. He couldn't believe the woman he'd been thinking about for months sat right under his nose at his— his father's—company. During a routine conference call, Rodney had mentioned *his* new overqualified coordinator, a transplant from North Carolina.

Confident, Rodney believed that in time he'd be able to have her takeover the national program, which could help them with other problems Rodney had created. Jax was aware of Rodney's reputation and honestly, had been in search of a way to quietly correct it. But, when he heard the woman's name, he emailed his secretary to book a flight. There weren't a lot of women named Darling in the world. And this one he couldn't forget. And didn't want to!

Now that he was in town and she knew he was here, he had to figure out what to do next. He could hang around town and sit in on a few meetings. But aside from her, fixing Rodney's problem and to make sure Rodney's sights didn't land on her, there wasn't any reason for him to be in Memphis. He would just have to manufacture something.

Hunched over his laptop at the small desk tucked along

a window of his hotel, The Peabody, he stared at the screen. For a moment or two, he surfed around without any real goal. Frustrated, he slapped the machine closed and strolled over to the bed and stretched out. Unable to do any work without thinking about her, for a while, he just focused on nothing staring at the ceiling which was just as ornate as the historic lobby. The flash of the lights from Beale Street below pulled his attention. Shit, he'd stayed in the same hotel the night he met her.

He ripped his tie from his neck and tossed it to the floor beside his jacket. A forty-two year old man who owned his own successful company shouldn't be sitting around in his hotel room fawning like a love-struck teenager over a woman he had one night with months ago.

Annoyed as hell at himself, he stripped the rest of his suit from his body dropping everything to the floor as he headed toward the bathroom. Hot shower and a stiff drink, then he would be able to push her out of his mind, until he saw her again tomorrow.

He leaned his head back into the spray from the nozzle. Warm and soothing, it flowed down his chest and he trailed it with a bar of soap. The touch of his hand to his body sprang memories of her to his mind.

Each stroke of his hand made the memory of her more vivid: the feel of her tongue, her mouth and the weight of her breasts in his hands. The images of her in his mind became more powerful and as they did, his body reacted. No matter how much or hard he massaged himself and begged for release, nothing worked. His hand couldn't replace the feel of her body. His head fell back against the wall behind him and his foot slipped. *Damn!* His ass hit the shower floor spring-boarding him back to reality.

What the hell was he doing?

He had to get this woman out of his head—or back into his bed.

CHAPTER THREE

"Hello, Mr. Slater," Darling greeted. At nearly a whisper, her voice betrayed her. Nothing about its meekness implied strength or self-assuredness. *Get it together woman!* Controlling her body's reaction to him felt like a battle she would continue to lose.

As his eyes locked on her and his mouth opened, Barbara floated through the door with an obvious purpose wearing a shirt cut too low and a skirt whose length was too short for work. "Hi, Mr. Slater."

But for once, Darling actually welcomed Barbara's presence. Otherwise, she would be forced to sit in a small closed room with the only man she'd been intimate with since moving to Memphis. A man whose freaking memory excited her body and made her crave his touch. She took a deep breath, inhaling that scent. *His* scent. It called to her and if Barbara weren't in the room, she couldn't be sure she wouldn't have responded just as she had before.

Jaxon rose from where he sat at a conference table to greet them. "Welcome, Darling, Barbara."

As they took their seats at the table, Darling was careful to take the seat farthest away without looking ridiculous.

"Rodney briefed me on where things stand for the remaining tradeshows this year." He turned toward Barbara. "Maybe we should begin with you, Barbara. Your team has done a great job organizing and managing our programs."

"Thank you." Barbara smiled. "My team can handle any increase in national meetings you think we should make."

"Thanks for being a team player. Rodney and I will definitely want to speak with you more about the calendar Darling developed and how we'll manage it moving forward."

"Mr. Slater—" Darling began. *What was he about to do?*

"Jaxon...please." His words were kind, but his eyes were serious.

"Barbara and I have been working together on national meetings and conferences since I came to work here. There's been such a crossover with some of the events that I identified as being strong opportunities to reach our customer—"

"Yes, sir," Barbara interrupted. "Events we identified as key to the company. We thought the two departments fit well together."

"Rodney and I agree with you." He moved some papers around, then handed them both an identical document. "Which is why I wanted to meet with you both here, to make you aware that there will be some changes."

A flash of heat washed over Darling and her palms began to sweat. The pen she held pressed deeper into the center of her hand as her grip tightened.

"Darling." His gaze was intense. "We've decided to combine your two workgroups." He turned his attention to the other woman. "Barbara, that means you'll report up to Darling."

"What?" Barbara asked, jumping up from her seat,

shoving back the chair. "I'm reporting to Darling? She's only been here for a few months. I've been here for years. What the hell is this? Where is Rodney—" Barbara stared at the door as if willing Rodney to appear, but he didn't.

Darling sat speechless, anger boiling inside of her. No one had told her the purpose of the reports she'd put together or of the meeting. A part of her thought he would even fire her because she'd walked away *that* night. He had the power to do it. Instead, he'd decided to obligate her to him and possibly humiliate her in the process.

"Rodney and I understand why this might be confusing for you." His voice was even, soothing. "This will not mean a change in your role or responsibilities."

"Then why this damn change?" Barbara asked, bitterly. The anger inside of her showed in the stiffness of her body. The woman who sashayed her way into the office had left, replaced with an angrier aggressive version.

He leaned in and locked his gaze onto Barbara's. "Rodney reports to me. In my opinion, with Darling's experience and knowledge, she will better manage the overall budget and strategy for identifying the best opportunities, which will take the company in the right direction." His voice didn't change, but there was no question who controlled the room.

Barbara folded her arms across her chest. "So, I have no option, but to accept this?"

"No." He touched another folder that rested on his desk. "You could take the option in this envelope."

Barbara glared at the thick envelope beneath his hand. She crumpled the paper she held into a ball and tossed it into a nearby trashcan. At the door, she turned and glared at them both.

The singe of her stare filled Darling with guilt. Darling hated managing the call center. This new job would be perfect. She had the experience and knew what to do. But, she didn't want it if it meant she had to sleep with her boss to keep it. Darling glanced behind her to make sure

Barbara was gone before she spoke, "Jaxon, does this have anything to do with us?" The words fell from her mouth before she could stop them. She wanted the answer to be no, but how could it be when he didn't know anything about her.

How could he make such a decision, just from my reports?

He walked to the door and closed it before he spoke. "No."

Alone in a room with a man she'd avoided for months, Darling knew she needed to keep her focus on her question, not her memories of how he looked naked. Or, the feel of his arms wrapped around her. Or, the faraway look in his eyes when he had an orgasm. All of it made her body ache to see and feel it again.

She stood to leave.

"This time you don't get to walk away."

His drawl was like warm molasses. She shivered. "Can you swear to me that this change has nothing to do with...that night?"

From where he sat, his eyes rolled over her entire body. Briefly, they paused on her breasts.

Her nipples perked in anticipation. She folded her arms across her chest in a weak attempt to conceal their betrayal.

His eyes met her gaze. "Yes. I can. This is my family's business. I'm not going to jeopardize it for anyone." He motioned for her to return to her seat and he moved to sit beside her. "Rodney's inappropriate relationship with Barbara has tied my hands a bit. But, he's wanted to replace her for a while. I thought this might be a good way to take care of everything without raising questions."

"And what if—"

"What if what?" You left me with nothing but questions...then I find out that you work for me." He leaned forward resting his forearms on the conference table.

"Nothing. Everything that happened was a mistake."

Just as she'd known it would be.

"Mistake?" He frowned.

"I just moved back to Memphis a few months ago, and I'm not trying to lose my job. But, I don't need to keep it by sleeping with the boss. That's not the kind of woman I am." There was no way she was about to find herself dating a wealthy man who would get his kicks, and then when he was tired... toss her to the side and find someone else to take her place.

He leaned back and to the left—away—resting his forearm on the armrest of the chair where he sat. It took him a moment to speak. "What have I done to make you think that's the kind of person I am?"

"You just gave me a promotion for no reason," she pointed out.

"I gave you a promotion because Rodney and I wanted to reorganize the structure of his group without creating a problem with Barbara. And because you deserved it based on your track record and experience."

"That's all?" she asked.

"That's all."

"What now?" she asked.

"I don't know." He paused. "I admit...I've thought of you a lot since that night."

"Me or my body?" She knew the answer to that question. The only thing he knew about her was her body.

"That's not fair. I gave you my number, but you never used it. You didn't give us...me a chance to know anything else."

There was really no reason for her to continue to sit and have this stupid conversation. He would say anything to cover his butt and get what he wanted. No matter what happened, it would end the same way. He was her boss, and now he was off limits. She stood again to leave. "I should get back to my desk."

"You're good at walking away." There was a noticeable edge to his voice.

"There's no reason for me to stay," she insisted.

The heels of Barbara's shoes cut through the thin carpet beneath them. She grabbed her purse from the cabinet above her desk and zeroed in on Rodney.

Who were they to treat her as if she was some unimportant new hire? She'd worked for this company for too many years to be kicked to the side for the new fresh face. If Rodney planned on having her in his bed again or didn't want his wife to find out she'd been there, he'd better fix this and fast.

The door to Rodney's office was open and the room dark.

"Kathy, have you seen Rodney?"

Kathy's head darted out from her cubicle. Her all too innocent eyes were always the same, clueless. Even when she and Rodney had sex in his office, the woman had been unaware. "Yeah, he said he had a family emergency and had to leave for the rest of the day."

"Thanks." She turned and flipped open her phone as she walked. "Rodney, call me back."

She slammed a tight small fist against the automatic door opener and stomped into the bright afternoon sun.

If they wanted a fight, she'd give them one.

No matter how many times Jaxon played back Darling's words in his head, he knew she was right. He was her boss and there wasn't anything that was going to change about that anytime soon.

Jaxon eased down the marble steps into the warm waters of the hotel's pool. A quick full-body dip into the heated water and he pushed off. The power of his legs and the precision of his hands slicing through the water drove his body forward. Lap after lap, he looped the pool until the muscles in his body cramped. He was thankful for the ache because it took his mind off Darling, if only for a brief moment. He kept swimming until his arms and legs felt anchored with liquid mercury. Elvis's familiar voice sang at him as he exited the water with no more answers than when he entered.

No woman had ever intrigued him the way Darling had. He'd planned it that way. But, now that he'd met her, something had changed.

He wanted her.

Trailing droplets behind him, he headed back to his room. Nothing outside of Darling quitting or his firing her would put them in a situation any different from the shit Rodney had created with Barbara.

CHAPTER FOUR

Pissed, Barbara sat on the hotel bed waiting for Rodney to arrive. She drank her wine a little too quickly and choked. The oaky tasting liquor burned her throat as she gasped. She released an angry exhale as her throat cooled. But, her earlier conversation with her sister riled her all over again. So what if she wasn't married? So what if she didn't have kids? It didn't mean a thing. She wasn't a stay-at-home mom like her sister. She worked for a living and even if she had to play the game a little, she could've done it without Rodney, if she'd had the chance.

What in the hell did Pat know about anything?

Pat was the kid her parents' loved more. They may never admit it, but they didn't have to say it out loud. It was written all over their faces at every family dinner or trip. Even at church. They always saved a seat for Pat, Ray—her husband, and their son. If Barbara showed up late, she had to grab a seat wherever she found one.

Her sister, like any other good Southern girl married her high-school sweetheart. They lived near the Mississippi

River in Harbortown. Because living in Midtown or Germantown wasn't good enough for Pat. No, they had to live on an island connected by a bridge to Memphis. Harbortown had its own grocery stores, shopping center, bars and restaurants. They didn't have to cross the bridge unless they were coming to visit her or their parents.

Barbie, you have such a cute little home. That's all Pat had to say when Barbara moved to Germantown and invited the family over for dinner.

Again, she checked her watch. It'd been thirty minutes since she'd spoken to Rodney. She rose and checked herself out in the mirror. Rodney bought the negligee she wore as a birthday present last year. She might be a little plumper, but she was still too hot for him. Smoothing her dark hair along her pale shoulders, she planned what she would say to him and their night.

She tossed back the last swallow of wine in her glass to calm the shivers running up and down her spine at the thought of spending another night with the fat freak. Unfortunately, jobs like hers were hard to find in Memphis and she had no desire to start over again.

Nine years. That's how long she'd been with the company. Right out of college, she'd taken the job with a starting salary higher than any of her friends. What kind of loser would she be if she had to search for a job—in this economy—while everyone else was building families and buying big second homes in the best parts of town?

What would Pat and her parents think of her?

Failure. That's what.

The clicks of the hotel door cued her to refill her glass and fill Rodney's.

"Hey, baby." He slid his tongue over his lower lip as he let his eyes travel her body.

His smile made her skin crawl. She gulped her wine. "Hey, handsome." She forced the words. "What took you so long?"

"My damn wife had a million questions." He threw his

jacket on the bed and quickly disrobed, displaying his huge stomach and too small briefs. Taking the glass of wine she offered, he reached for her breast. He squeezed them as if he was testing a cantaloupe for ripeness.

She swiped his hand away. "Baby, you know I like that, but first, we need to talk—"

He reeked of skunky beer. His mouth covered hers, wet and sloppy as usual. When he mumbled his way down her neck, he left an unpleasant trail of saliva. "We'll talk later."

Pushing at the soft flesh of his chest, Barbara stepped back. "Unless you want your wife to ask a million more questions," she spat angrily, "we need to talk, now." Then, she forced a smile. She didn't want to piss him off before she got what she wanted.

"What?" A stunned look of disbelief slowly crawled across his face. "Why would you do that?"

Adjusting her boobs to show him just what he might never have again, she went on, "I've been calling you since my meeting this morning and you didn't respond." She slapped her glass down on the table beside her. "Why would you agree to those changes—?"

"I didn't agree to anything," he yelled. "You're putting my marriage in jeopardy playing this kind of childish game!"

"I'm not playing games with you. You promised me, Rodney." She blinked her eyes, shocked that tears blurred her vision. Of all the stupid things. She'd begun to cry. Where was the control she needed?

"You're fucking up my career and my marriage, *and* you're crying?" He ran his fingers through the thinning hair on his head before pulling it free and slapping it against his leg.

"What about my career?" she demanded, hands on her hips.

He had no response.

Bastard!

She swiped the tears from her eyes. "Don't worry about my tears. Just worry about this…" She let her robe fall, and stripped the negligee from her body.

His anger disappeared as he drank in the sight of her breasts and hips. "Please." He grabbed her hand, and put it on his crotch. "I want you."

He'd give her what she wanted one way or another. What he'd promised.

Closing her eyes, she allowed him to lead her to the bed.

Jaxon's tongue slid up the length of her neck, slowly. The longer he took to reach her mouth, the more Darling craved the touch of his lips to hers. She wound her fingers into the short locks of his hair and pulled him tighter to her neck.

He sucked harder as he pushed himself deeper inside of her.

The stronger and deeper his thrusts, the more her body became his.

Jaxon raised his mouth from her neck and suddenly, his beautiful eyes were locked on hers. He dipped his head closer and closer.

It was taking forever. All she wanted was to feel his lips against hers. Something was wrong. Instead of getting closer, he'd begun to pull away. What was happening?

No!

She tightened her grip, but nothing worked.

Darling's eyes sprang open. Jolted from her sleep again, this time she was thankful. The dreams of Jaxon that'd been filling her nights were becoming too powerful to fight and too often, she woke angry that they hadn't been real. They—he—always felt so real. Her body obviously couldn't tell the difference because it responded every time. She'd taken to locking her bedroom door at night because she didn't know if she was acting out the dreams in her sleep. But, from the look of the sheets twisted around her body, she had to be participating.

Reaching beneath the covers, she untangled her satiny gown. As she ran her hands along the soft fabric, she smiled. What was she doing dressing for her dream-lover? She smoothed the covers around her, flipped the sweaty pillow to the dry side and lay back in bed. The train thundered along the tracks behind her parents' house. Its power rattled the metal case she had sitting against the wall beside her bed.

Memories of her childhood danced through her head as she listened to the strange music around her. She remembered playing in the backyard while her mother hung clothes outside. That was before her parents could afford to buy a washer and dryer. *Before her mother got a good job.*

They never had a ton of money, just enough to not be poor. As soon as she could leave, she did. Now she was back and this time, she had no real idea of when she would be able to leave again. She'd been gone so long it was weird to be back. She felt so different from the child who had left, but not different enough. Not different enough for Jaxon. As she sat listening to the roar of the train, she knew her ex was right. Sometimes, it's best to put some things behind you. She just never thought her ex would ever think that way about her.

The scream of the train's whistle quieted and she turned over, pulling the covers over her head. She welcomed the heavy weight of her eyelids.

But, as she wrapped her arms around her pillow and snuggled deeper, her alarm sounded, chasing away sleep and dreams of Jaxon.

Jaxon's beautiful bright smile greeted Darling as she

walked into her office. "Good morning," he said.

He'd filled her nights and now, he sat watching her. She needed coffee or something to handle seeing him first thing in the a.m. "Morning." She dropped her purse on the corner of her desk and tried to control her thoughts as she sat. "Did we have an appointment?"

"No, but I thought maybe we should talk a little more about the changes."

She turned on her computer and began to click in her passwords. She welcomed the distraction, and tried her best to focus on anything other than him, and the persimmon scent filling her office. He smelled the same as he did in her dreams. How was that possible? "Okay, sure...just let me—"

"No, not now, I thought maybe lunch or dinner." He waited.

She rummaged around her desk for something. Her fingers touched the stapler before she realized that was stupid. Again, she clicked away at her keyboard. He couldn't see her. He didn't know she was typing in nothing because she couldn't focus. "Uhh, I don't know about dinner." There was no way she would be able to sit in some dimly lit restaurant staring into his eyes while eating. A few of her dreams included whipped cream and some well-placed strawberries. She would never make it through dessert.

The smile that flashed across his face told her he knew exactly why she said no to dinner. "Lunch, then."

"Lunch. Yeah—that would be okay." The freaking teenager inside her choked on her words. *Why did this man keep scrambling her brain?*

"Then, let's say one o'clock." He stood to leave.

The man took his sweet time leaving. Every move seemed calculated to capture her attention and she enjoyed it. "Okay," she agreed.

The moment he left, Darling flopped back in her chair. How on earth would she make it through lunch with this man? Between her dreams and reality, there was no escape. She paused before inhaling a long deep breath. *He smelled so damn good!*

She needed to splash a little water on her face to cool herself off.

The water from the bathroom faucet could not run cold enough to cool the images of him in her mind or the memories of his touch heating her body. No matter how many times she dipped her face into the cool water in her hands, nothing helped.

The sound of sniffles drew her attention. "Hello?" Only one of the stalls had a closed door. Obviously, whoever it was had hidden there for privacy and her presence was an intrusion.

No answer.

She walked over to the stall that had shoes visible. Gorgeous tan shoes with red trim and a four inch heel. *Barbara.* "Are you okay?"

Again, no answer.

She waited and finally the door opened. Barbara walked out. "Mind your own damn business."

"Barbara, I'm sorry about all this." Darling dabbed her hands against her skirt.

"Sure you are." The woman's voice held an edge of bitterness. She didn't have to say anything else. Her stiff jaw and piercing glare said it all. Barbara swiped at her tears.

Despite her words, the pain in her eyes made Darling want to soothe her. The woman could be a pain in the butt, but nobody should be hiding in the bathroom crying. Then, Darling's brain clicked into gear. Barbara's fear didn't have anything to do with her. The woman had screwed the boss, that disgusting idiot Rodney. Apparently, it hadn't done her much good and she realized she'd taken the wrong one to bed. If she had the chance, she knew Barbara would correct that mistake. Then, somebody else, maybe even Darling, would be the one in the bathroom crying. "I had nothing to do with any of this." She didn't know what else to say. It was the truth as far as she knew.

"Really?" Barbara dabbed at her red nose. "Why would you say that? What are you hiding?"

I slept with the boss. Just like you! "Nothing. I'm concerned—"

"Then why has Jaxon taken such a liking to you?" Barbara didn't bother to look directly at her, but instead asked her question to the mirror in front of her as she glared at Darling's reflection.

She should've just left. Trying to be nice, now the woman stared at her trying to figure out her secret. "What do you mean by that?"

Barbara spun around to face her. "Since he arrived, he seems to only have one thing on his mind. You."

"That's not true." And if it were, how would she know.

"Rodney told me that he's fixated with you." She blew her nose. "He said that it's all about you."

"That's not true. I don't think Rodney would say that." Had she or Jaxon done anything to give away what happened between them? Had they given Rodney any clues? "Everything he knows about me, he knows from Rodney."

"Listen, you little bitch." She tossed the make-up and tear soaked tissue into the trash. "If you think you can beat me at this game, think again."

Stunned by the entire conversation, Darling watched the woman storm from the bathroom. What in the hell did Barbara mean by, *all about you*?

*

CHAPTER FIVE

Table linens fluttered and restaurant patrons stared, as Darling stormed across the restaurant. But, the woman heading toward him excited Jaxon, even if she made him nervous. And today wasn't the first time. From their first night together, she intimidated him, a little. No woman had ever been as direct, or as dismissive. He drank from the glass in front of him as he flashed back on the night she had him trailing through the hotel room behind her…butt naked.

Ridiculous.

What woman would want a man that didn't have the balls to stand his ground with her?

The beautiful features of her face were blank, except her eyes. Anger clear and distinct flashed from them. "You lied to me," she accused when she reached his table.

"Lied?" he questioned. "About what?"

She slammed an envelope down in front of him. "With everything that's going on, you've left me no other option."

He picked up the envelope. He didn't need to open it because the knot in his gut told him what it held. "I haven't lied to you about anything. Ever." He ripped the letter in half. "I don't need this, and you can't quit." She could, but he wouldn't allow it. He stuffed the torn pieces into his suit pocket, and forced himself to remain calm. "Sit down."

"I have to go." She stared at his pocket, while she bit at her bottom lip. "I did what I came to do."

Whatever would or wouldn't happen between them would be determined by them. No one would fill her head with lies. "Sit down, Darling."

She hesitated, but finally she nodded her head and lowered herself into the chair. "Why did you do this to me?"

"I haven't done anything to you." He reached for her hand, but she snatched it away. "Tell me what you think you know." He slid the glass of water near her hand.

"What I know is that I saw Barbara crying in the bathroom." She lifted her glass of water and sipped. "And she told me that Rodney told her that you're '…all about me.' That what happened to her is because of me. Us. You."

"Rodney told her that?" Rodney didn't know a damn thing. Jaxon felt certain of that much. If Barbara knew anything, she'd guessed it.

"Yes." She crunched ice from her glass of water. "I need this job, but I won't screw you or screw Barbara over to keep it."

He thought for a second. "Screw? Is that what we did?" It was beginning to feel like it was a hell of a lot more. Because he didn't know how to explain anything he'd done since that night. He'd even done an online search her *Darling, North Carolina* and found her bio from her old job. He was sure Rodney had hired her because she was beautiful, but she was probably more qualified than Rodney to run the damn division.

"Jaxon, please. Don't."

"Don't what, Darling? I'm only asking you a question." The plea in her eyes cut right through him because he knew exactly how she felt. Shit! For now, he would walk away from it. "Okay, Darling, for now," he continued, "Rodney doesn't know anything about me, you, or why I'm here." His anger and dislike for Rodney flared as he saw the hurt in her eyes. "I've had no conversations with Rodney outside of our meetings regarding the merger of your two workgroups." He waited. "Nothing. I promise you."

"Then, why would Rodney tell her that?"

He had one guess and he was sure he was right. "Rodney and Barbara have had a relationship for years."

"I know." She twisted her mouth in distaste.

"That relationship has secured a lot of opportunities for Barbara and a lot of sex for Rodney," he continued, "Rodney's covering his ass with her."

"And using me as a scapegoat."

The anger in her voice faded, but was quickly replaced with irritation. He hoped it was directed at Rodney and not at him. He kept his gaze on her face. "Sounds like it."

"Either way, I don't want to be caught in the middle of all of this." She took one last long drink of water.

Jaxon watched as her tongue darted out and pulled one of the ice cubes between her full sensuous lips. The droplets from the ice cubes moistened her lips distracting him from his thoughts.

The sound of the cubes of ice crunching stopped, and she spoke, "I'm only interested in my work, not being a part of stupid office politics." She pushed her chair back and stood.

"I'll take care of this." Hell, he had no idea how to get Darling either out of his mind, or into his bed. But, without knowing it, Rodney was fucking up his plans.

###

No matter how badly she needed this job or any job, Darling wasn't going to let it, or Jaxon, hold her hostage. He may not have accepted her resignation, but she still planned to start applying for jobs as soon as she got back to her parents' house. The minute she found something—anything, she would quit, and he wouldn't be able to stop her.

She gave herself kudos for saying what she had to say and getting it off her chest. But, her growling stomach didn't agree with her decision to do it before she ate. Sitting at the counter at The Arcade, a historic landmark, the oldest restaurant in Memphis, she ran through the scene again in her mind. She wanted desperately to forget the look of disappointment in Jaxon's beautiful green eyes as she stood to walk away.

He'd ripped the letter that she'd so painfully typed into pieces without even reading it. A small part of her tingled with happiness that he tore it up, but the part of her that was pissed at Rodney, Barbara and Jaxon didn't like it one bit.

While she waited on her food, she called the only friend she had. At least the only one she still had after the divorce. The others all seemed to disappear with Steve.

With the click of the line, she asked, "Hey, what are you doing?"

"Trying to get out the door," Annette responded.

At least somebody had a life. She could live vicariously. "Where're you off to?"

"Going out with that guy I told you about the other day." There was a rustle of something in the background. "I don't even know why I'm even putting in so much effort."

"You don't sound too excited." She knew her friend was probably spinning in front of her mirror checking out her appearance. Maybe trying to determine which shoe worked better with her outfit. If nothing else, Annette was definitely fashion conscious. "Maybe you should stay home and go out on a different day when you feel more like it."

"Um, I don't know. I guess it's more about men not putting in much effort. Like this guy. Can you tell me why he prefers to text vs. talk?" Annette sighed. "He has my number why doesn't he use it?"

"Are you really asking the divorcee with no prospects about men?" It was almost too pathetic. She inhaled the plate of food placed in front of her. "You may not like the choices in front of you, but at least you have options."

"I guess that's one way to look at it," Annette continued, "I'm about to hop on the elevator. If I lose you, I'll call you right back. But, anyway, what's up?"

"Not much." She loaded her fork with fried okra. "I thought I'd call and let you know that you were right."

"About what?" The elevator dinged softly in the background.

"Jaxon ripped up my resignation letter."

Annette laughed. "Anybody could've told you that would happen."

"What am I supposed to do? Sit around and wait for him or his lackey to fire me because I won't screw the boss?"

The woman sitting further down the counter looked up from her magazine at Darling.

"Why do you think that'll happen?" Annette asked.

Embarrassment made her lower her voice, "I don't know." She could admit she might have a few issues with men. "Isn't that how these things always go? They get tired of you and trade you in?" Her relationship with Steve had been her longest. She knew he had his ways, but she didn't think he would leave her.

"Sounds like you're talking about Steve, not Jaxon," Annette said. "Look, you need the job and until you find another one, quitting isn't an option."

How different were the two men?

No matter how much she didn't like hearing what Annette said, she was right. Quitting wasn't an option because she was too old to live with her parents. She needed her job, or another one. Her credit was crap. It would take her even longer to get back on her feet if she had to start all over again. "Well, when everything finalizes from my divorce, I'll have some money. That'll help a lot."

Why did divorcing a lying cheating jerk take so long? The judge should just say cheaters give the one cheated on everything they want. Done. Finished.

"Yeah, but you don't have it now. And right now, you have to eat."

It didn't matter how much she wanted Annette to be wrong, she was right. Even her fifteen dollar meal was a splurge she really couldn't afford, but she didn't feel like going back to work. And she didn't want to deal with her parents' curious looks and unasked questions if she came home early. They meant well, but sometimes, they still treated her like a little girl. "Eating is overrated." She loaded up another forkful of food.

"Is this really about the job?" Annette asked, laughing softly. "Or about the fact that the man is gorgeous and you can't stop thinking about him?"

"What do you know? Who said I can't stop?" If Annette knew about her dreams, she'd have absolutely no leverage what-so-ever.

"You did." She laughed, again. "I'll call you back later. I'm about to hop on the train."

Darling popped the trunk of her car, carefully reached in and pulled out the wedding dress that for some reason, she hadn't been able to part with. The lace and beads were hand-stitched. Back then, she weighed about twenty pounds less. She remembered with pain the day she saw the dress. She'd been out lunching with her mother and

Annette. After lunch, they did some window shopping. When they passed the bridal shop, they all looked at each other with one thought. What the heck, why not take a look? Who knew they'd actually find something. The moment they saw it, they knew it was *the one*. The thing was she'd bought it before Steve had proposed.

Annette stored the dress at her house for months until Steve actually asked her to marry him. Now the thought made her laugh. Maybe that should've been her first clue that there was something crazy going on with her. She had been absolutely obsessed with him since they first met. No one could ever live up to the type of fantasy she'd created.

She put the dress back into her trunk. As soon as she could, she'd put it back in storage. Instead, she grabbed the other bags of clothes she no longer had a need for: evening gowns, shoes and extravagant purses, then walked into the consignment store to make her monthly drop off. Plus, she could use a few more reasonably priced suits. They always had a great selection.

An hour later, with cash and new suits in hand, Darling drove the streets of Memphis with no place to go. The city seemed strange and different, now. Her high school friends were just that. They were so far apart in who they were now that it made it difficult for them to relate. And her family, her parents, she didn't want them to know how far she'd fallen, because she and Steve couldn't agree on anything. Every extra dollar went to her lawyers and her part of the mortgage until things were finalized.

Just how had that happened? He left her! Why did she have to continue to pay the mortgage?

For some reason, she ended up in front of her high school.

Her high school had been a big deal when she was a kid with both a junior high and high school on the same campus. They provided more college preparatory classes than any other public school back then. Now, the junior high was some type of weird annex and the grounds didn't look as beautiful as she'd remembered. Through the eyes of a child, she'd thought the place was huge. Because she'd taken the bus to school, it seemed like it was on the other side of the world. But, it was only about fifteen minutes from her parents' house. And now, it seemed small and old. Falling apart.

Just like me

She looked over at the bags resting on the seat beside her and cried.

CHAPTER SIX

The he stench of the weight room at the hotel—an odd mix of sweat and rubber—didn't bother Jaxon as he loaded more weight onto the bar. A weird sense of relief flowed through him as he laid across the bench and braced himself for what was to come. He gripped the warm metal and forced the bar to move with his will as much as his strength. The ache in his muscles increased with each pump and he welcomed it every time. Sweat rolled down his arms dripping onto his face. Into his eyes.

He rested the weights and grabbed his towel to wipe away his perspiration. As soon as he dropped the towel back to its resting place, images of Darling flooded him again. Nothing he did allowed him to push thoughts of her out of his mind. *Damn!* The metallic ringing and the grunting sounds of the men and women tackling the weights around him alerted him. He sat, doing nothing. The mirror across the way reflected what he already knew. This woman knocked him off his game and he needed to figure out why.

After unsuccessfully trying to focus, Jaxon gave up on the weights and hit the showers.

Just as he reached his car, his phone rang. "Hello."

"Hey, it's your mom."

"Mom, I know it's you." He laughed. She'd only been using a cell phone for a few months and wasn't very tech savvy. She kept forgetting her cell number would show on his screen.

"Oh, sorry. I forgot." She paused. "How much longer do you think you'll be in Memphis?"

"I'm not sure. There are some things I'm trying to straighten out down here." He knew he was lying to himself, more than to her.

"Is there a lot wrong?" she asked with concern.

"No, ma'am," he assured her. "I've decided to restructure one of the departments and I want to make sure it's handled smoothly."

"I know you will take care of it." She paused. "You've made the company more successful than even your father did when he was alive."

That may be true, but it wasn't something he'd done intentionally. He'd fired many of his father's cronies because he didn't like them and they'd shielded his father and his cheating from his mother. The increase in sales was a benefit, but unexpected. Apparently, his father's most trusted board and executives had been screwing him while his father was whoring around. "Thanks mom. I think things will be better soon."

"Well, I've been nominated for an award." Her voice was filled with barely controlled excitement. "They're going to announce the winners at the Women of Excellence dinner."

His parents divorced when he was a child and since that time, there had been only two things his mother had dedicated herself to: him and volunteering. When he left for college, her home was empty and it broke her heart because she feared he would never return. He'd actually thought about it. But, when his father died, someone had to take over the family business. That was six years ago. Each year, it grew harder for him to walk in his father's footsteps, but it was important to his mother. So, even if it had been hands-off for the most part, a Slater ran Slater Enterprises.

At the reading of the will, he met the stewardess his father had left them for. However, he'd never begun a new family with her. Her disappointment at the reading of the will was obvious. Bitterness filled him as he remembered how she'd then come on to every other man in the room.

"Women of Excellence," he repeated. "That sounds like a big deal."

"Oh, it is, and I'd love for my successful handsome son to be my escort."

He couldn't remember the last time his mother had been on a date, or mentioned a man, romantically. He and his father owed her. His father broke her hear, and Jaxon had become her whole heart. She deserved more— grandchildren—to love and spoil. He'd been so busy *living* that he hadn't thought much about her or anyone else. Definitely not as far as starting a family. "Of course, mom." He smiled into the phone. "When?"

"March 10th. But, I want to be sure you put it on your calendar."

"I'll be there." It was a promise he couldn't break. She was the only woman he'd ever been able to be completely honest with. No matter what he did or didn't do, she stood beside him. How could his father ever have left a woman so beautiful and kind? How could the damn man have left his son? What kind of husband or father would he make with a role model like that?

"And maybe you can wear one of your wonderful dark suits with a green shirt to match your eyes. I'll wear a full-length gown." She paused. "We'll have a glorious time."

53

Jaxon paused before he walked into the staff meeting. Rumors about why the two groups were merging had swirled around the office. Rodney reported them all, partly because of his concern for his own job and because he seemed to like gossip.

People were sitting in groups according to their respective divisions. He did however, notice a few of Barbara's group had defected to the so-called enemy blending with Darling and her staff.

"Hello everyone." He paused. "Before we get started, let me say I appreciate everyone in this room for what you've contributed to the company. And although there'll be some reporting differences, there will be no job losses."

A shared sigh breezed through the room. Stiff tense postures relaxed as people waited to hear what he'd say next.

"Collectively, your units contribute more than thirty percent to the company's numbers. With this realignment, we're hoping to be able to increase that." When he finished with what he had to say, he turned the room over to Rodney and Darling.

While Rodney spoke, his words seemed to be directed specifically to Barbara.

As a contrast, Darling's focus had been more on the direction of the department going forward, and her desire to keep confusion to a minimal during the transition.

Jaxon noticed that Barbara glowered in a corner throughout Rodney's entire speech. Women like her and the stewardess, that caused Jaxon's father to break his mother's heart, were never satisfied. He could've fired her and promoted someone else into a modified position, but Rodney had begged him not to.

Even though she still had a job, she sat in obvious unhappiness, filled with resentment and anger.

Not sure of what he might see, he chanced a quick look at Darling. Surrounded by staff from both units, he allowed himself the opportunity to watch.

She moved her gaze from one person to another as they vied for her attention, her long black hair brushing her shoulders each time she turned her head.

As the crowd dwindled away, he caught her eye. The beautiful smile she gave him warmed him with its intensity. Then, with a tiny nod, she broke eye contact and focused on the people around her.

He felt the loss of contact immediately, its warmth replaced with pain. Something was going on between them and he couldn't let go of it.

Whatever *it* was, it grew stronger each time he was around her. Not fading away.

###

Darling watched as Jaxon ducked out of the room, leaving her with her new team. Everyone congratulated her, except Barbara, who practically ran from the room.

As soon as Jaxon finished speaking, after slapping Darling on the back and a quick handshake, Rodney left too.

Maybe the whole thing wouldn't be as bad as she'd originally thought. If Barbara could accept the changes and not provoke any problems, everything might just be okay. Feeling pretty good, Darling headed toward Rodney's office to ask a few questions. Some of her new team members hadn't had their travel schedules approved for the remainder of the year and that needed to be done if she was going to begin working on her end of year budget.

Darling stopped at the sound of voices coming from Rodney's office, their tones were hushed and angry

"Rodney, this is BS!" No mistaking Barbara's voice.

"Baby, calm down." There was a pause. "We'll figure this out together."

"This is your fault," she raged. "She comes in from nowhere and suddenly, I'm reporting to her. No way in hell!"

"Baby, she does have a lot of experience. The two departments should be together. It makes a lot of sense."

"Then why doesn't she report to me?" Barbara demanded.

"Her department is doing better—"

"I don't care," she interrupted. "I've been here longer."

"Mr. Slater reviewed the numbers and made the final decision. Shit, Barbara, the economy is bad. We could've lost jobs, but we didn't."

"I don't care. I'm not reporting to her."

The voices stopped and Darling attempted to flatten herself against the wall behind her.

Barbara stormed from the office, and bolted down the hallway.

As she watched the angry figure stomp down the hall, she knew Barbara would soon become a bigger pain in the butt. She didn't have anything against the woman, but clearly, Barbara wasn't going to just accept the new structure. If the woman searched around enough who knew what she'd find. If the night she and Jaxon spent together was discovered, it could hurt his company—him. Or, Barbara could leverage her relationship with Rodney to ruin the company.

Jaxon should've done something about it a long time ago, but his attempt to manage the company from a distance had allowed his absence to be manipulated. Darling may not have had anything to do with it, but if she stayed, this would definitely become more about her than anything else.

CHAPTER SEVEN

Darling sat in the coffee shop of the bookstore people watching. The older gentleman that eased onto the bar stool beside her glanced at the menu briefly before ordering. Darling couldn't take her eyes off the man and not because he rivaled Sean Connery. His tight thin lipped expression as he sat stiffly reviewing the menu gave him an unapproachable air. As he read the menu, his eyes darted across everyone at the counter, not long enough to establish contact with anyone, but as if searching for something—someone.

God, was that going to be her life, now? Would that be her future? Would she turn into him?

While he waited for his food order, he shoved his hands into his pockets and ambled through the aisles. Now and then, he'd pause to read the back cover copy of books.

Although her own marriage had been a failure, her parents had been together forever. Her parents lived their own lives, but spent as much time as possible together too. Maybe there was no reason for her sadness over the jacket-clad older man. Maybe his wife waited at home for him to return.

Darling closed her eyes to block out the sight of him. When she opened them, he stood next to her checking out his order: one pork chop and a side of greens with a roll. Definitely not enough to share.

Would she one day, at sixty-five or seventy, stroll through the aisles of bookstores or order lunch or dinner dressed in her afternoon best because she had no one to go home to? Would strangers become her only friends?

The weeks since his conversation with his mother passed with a blur. He didn't know if his time in Memphis moved quickly because of the work he was doing, or if it was because he tried to squeeze every moment out of every day he spent near Darling.

The forty-five minute flight to Nashville didn't give Jaxon enough time to catch a nap before he met his mother. He raced from the plane straight to the car waiting for him. There hadn't been much need to bring any luggage since he was hopping right back on a plane to Memphis when the event was over. He might not be able to be *with* Darling when he returned, but he could be near her.

He had no idea how long he could stretch out his stay in Memphis, but he'd done a good job of it so far. Something about Rodney and Barbara convinced him that as soon as he was out of sight, Darling might have more problems than she could handle. Of course, if she knew he extended his stay because of her, he felt sure she would be irritated.

The driver dropped him at his condo, then he jumped into his car and kept going. He knew his phone would ring soon, because his plane arrived a little late, and Elaine Slater was always punctual. As he swiped the card to open the gate to his mother's community, his phone rang. He smiled as he answered it.

"Yes, ma'am."

"Honey, where are you?" his mother asked.

"We won't be late." He knew that was her unasked question. "Pulling up in a minute."

"Well, don't park, I'll be right out."

"Okay."

The retirement community where his mother lived provided everything she could possibly need. Landscapers cared for each lawn, a community organizer arranged neighborhood events and his mother had regular engagements with neighbors. The neighborhood resembled any other affluent Nashville community, except you rarely saw children during the week. Grandchildren usually only visited on the weekend.

As he navigated the winding well-loved streets, he wondered how his mother managed the twists and turns in the darkness when he had problems himself. He turned from one street named after a plant to another street named after another plant until he neared his mother's house. Eventually, he would have to talk her into moving out of the huge empty home to something smaller and closer to him. The door to his mother's home opened just as he pulled up.

His mother looked gorgeous. The tasteful green dress she'd chosen fit her petite frame. Her beautiful silver hair was cut into a short bob that highlighted her high cheekbones.

Jaxon hopped out to grab her door. "Mom, you look beautiful." He kissed her on the cheek.

A slight pink colored her cheeks. "Thank you."

After he slid back into the driver's seat, he asked, "Who nominated you for the award?"

A smile crossed her face. "Different civic organizations throughout Nashville nominated people they knew to be doing good work in the communities."

"So, you didn't have to bribe anyone." He winked.

The look on his mother's face couldn't be described as anything other than priceless. Slowly, her face flushed. "I would never—"

"Mom, I'm joking. Relax." He laughed. "You are such a wonderful person. I'm surprised it took this long for someone to nominate you."

"You are so awful." She smiled.

"I'm proud of you, mom," he said. "You deserve this."

As they pulled up to the hotel where the event was being held, he kissed her on the cheek. "You are such an easy target." He laughed and handed the keys to the valet.

The woman Jaxon's mother led to the table wore a black evening gown that hugged her toned body well. Her blonde hair brushed the top of her tanned shoulders slightly. He rose from his chair as they neared.

"Honey, this is Melanie Jones," his mother told him. "She's volunteered with me in the past and was also nominated."

"Hi, Ms. Jones, nice to meet you." It never failed. At every event, his mother introduced him to some woman, a potential wife. He would never break his mother's heart and let her know that he always took advantage of each introduction. Just not the way she'd hoped. Some things you just didn't tell your mother.

"Please, Melanie is fine." She smiled.

"Honey, sit. I wanted Melanie to meet you because she's originally from Memphis and I know you've been spending a lot of time there."

"Your mom said you're working on some issues with your office in Memphis." Her voice was soft and pleasant.

"I think we have everything under control." He smiled to please his mother as much as he did her. "A little restructuring."

"It can't be under control because he hasn't come home, for good, yet," his mother said. "Melanie spends a lot of time in Memphis. Maybe you two can go to dinner or something while you're there."

"I'd love to if you have time, Jaxon." Melanie handed him a business card with her cell phone number.

If that card had been given to him a few months ago, he would've taken full advantage of it whenever the need arose. But, now, every time he closed his eyes, he was bombarded with images of the only woman he wanted—and the beautiful woman staring at him wasn't her. "I don't know how much longer I'll be there, but—"

"Of course, he has time for dinner," his mother interrupted. "Maybe I'll fly down and we can all make an evening of it.

Any other time and he would say yes. But right now, he didn't know what he was doing. Spending time with Melanie wouldn't make it any less complicated. "Mom, I don't think I'll be there for much longer."

"I haven't been to Memphis for a long time. I think it could be a lot of fun. We could see a play at the Orpheum. I used to love that theatre. Your father and I had season tickets."

He forgot how good his mother was at getting her way. "Okay. Okay. I give up. We'll plan it. Dinner and a show."

"I look forward to it," Melanie said.

"So do we," his mother replied.

The tiny little movie theater had quickly become one of Darling's favorites. It didn't show every movie that came out, but they served wine and cheese, so that put it on the top of her list. She chose a completely empty row, right in the middle of the small theatre and popped open her container of fruit.

"Hi."

His voice rolled over her as he sat in the seat beside her.

Darling patted her hand at her throat and coughed. After a quick sip of wine, she responded, "Hi." *What was he doing here?*

"No, I'm not following you," Jaxon said as if reading her mind. He tore off a piece of pretzel which smelled of cinnamon and sugar and popped it into his mouth. "You didn't see me when you walked in, but I thought I'd join you."

"Oh."

He stopped chewing. Not even the dim light of the theatre could hide the beauty or warmth of his eyes. "Is that okay? I can move if it's a problem."

The only thing Darling could do was watch his mouth as he spoke. She wondered how he would taste with a little cinnamon and sugar. "That's not necessary. We're adults."

He smiled and kept chewing as the lights dimmed.

The actor in the love scene on the screen lifted the actress' leg into the air and kissed her knee. The actor ran his mouth down the woman's leg followed by his fingers. The only thing Darling could think of was when did knees become sexy? God, she needed some air. "Excuse me for a minute." She ran to the bathroom like a teenager.

What's with me? Just because an attractive man sat beside her, smelling like—like a sexy male, didn't mean she had to immediately begin thinking of him with his clothes off. Honestly, she should just duck out of the theatre.

She reached for her keys.

Crap! She left her purse in her seat, reluctantly, she returned to the theatre. It would be childish to duck out now, but she wanted to run away from here. Away from Jaxon.

"Are you okay?" he asked, concern in his voice.

"Yeah." Did his voice always sound like that? Gravelly and…concerned?

"You sure?" He stared through the darkness right at

her.

The flicker of the movie screen highlighted those beautiful green eyes and the worry behind them.

He handed her the fruit and wine she'd practically thrown at him when she ran away. A flush of embarrassment flowed through her. There was more wine than she remembered and she was grateful. She took a long sip and sat back in her chair. She accepted that for the next hour or so, she was stuck in a chair beside a man whose attraction was slowly becoming more difficult for her to deny.

Before Darling ran from the theatre, Jaxon was about to do it himself. Sitting near her watching the actor on screen pretend to make love only brought back memories of his one night with her. It made him want to take her where she sat. His need to touch her, to hold her and kiss her grew with each pretend caress on the screen. The only thing that would help him was a cold shower or at least splashing some water on his face.

He walked out of the movie moments after she did to do just that. Even though he took the time to replace the wine and fruit she'd thrown at him, he still returned to their seats before she did. Maybe she was really sick, and didn't want to tell him.

No matter how much he tried to pay attention to the movie, he couldn't stop watching her. The more she laughed at the actors' antics, the more relaxed she became. When she laughed loudly, she muffled it with her hand.

His favorite moments were when something surprised her. She'd jump and lean into him just a little before pulling away. Each time, leaving the scent of fresh baked cake behind. Each time he wanted to grab her and stop her from moving away, but he didn't.

They sat until the credits were over, and the house

lights came up.

"Did you like it?" he asked.

"You couldn't tell?" She grinned. "I laughed so hard, I cried."

"I wasn't sure I'd like it, but it was good." The theatre had been practically empty before they entered and now, those few movie watchers had left. The cleaning staff had begun to sweep and prep for the next showing. "I guess we should leave and allow them to do their jobs."

"I guess so." Her tone didn't match her expression.

If they sat in the theatre any longer, eventually, someone would ask them to help clean or leave. He didn't want to let her go, not yet. "Darling, let's go next door for coffee or dessert?"

"I don't know. Do you think we should? With everything going on, I mean. Would that make sense?"

"Probably not. You're right. But, it's just coffee." He reaffirmed, hoping she'd give in.

"Only coffee." She smiled at him.

"I promise. No games or tricks."

"Just two co-workers having dessert." She paused. "Nothing's ever that simple. I'm sorry, Jaxon. Good night." She turned and walked away.

As he watched her, he knew she was right, but he also knew he wouldn't be able to let her go. The pain that stole his breath begged him to run after her and kiss her. Hold her. Make her listen to him, but the rational side of his brain told him not to move.

CHAPTER EIGHT

$\mathbf{B}$arbara parallel parked at the end of the block between a car with the hood up and another one missing tires and just sat there and watched. Darling pulled into the driveway, hopped out of her car and popped the trunk. *Who could she know in this neighborhood?* As Barbara checked the clock on her dashboard, she clicked her door locks one more time. This part of Memphis was nothing like where she lived. There weren't nearly enough street lights, and if anyone set up a make-shift mechanic shop on her street she was sure they would receive a citation from code enforcement and be told to move it out, quick.

Darling grabbed some bags out of the trunk of her car, then headed toward the front door of the brick house and unlocked it. What? Is this where she lived? Another car pulled in behind Darling's, and Barbara watched as Darling held the door for the older couple. After filling their arms with as many bags as they could carry, they ambled up to the front door overloaded.

Barbara sat until the stare of the middle-aged man

working under the hood of the car in front of her and the sunset made her uncomfortable. She decided sitting there made her too conspicuous and she should leave before someone asked any questions. But a hasty exit flew out the window when she turned the corner only to be caught by the red flashing lights and electronic gates halting traffic for the passing train. Her Range Rover didn't blend with the line of cars waiting on the train to pass.

Can't spy on someone like that. Next time, I'll get a rental car.

The drive to her part of town took forever even without traffic. As soon as she walked into her condo, she stripped her clothes off, tossed them onto a pile of laundry and lay naked across her bed.

Now what?

At the office, Darling dressed in designer clothes and flaunted stylish handbags as if she lived in Germantown somewhere. Instead, it turned out she lived with some old couple, probably her parents, in a neighborhood definitely not on the scale of Germantown. Why? What was she doing with her money?

I should've followed her weeks ago! Her entire body tingled with anticipation at her discovery. This was the best thing that had happened to her in a while. There was no way Jaxon Slater would be interested in a woman that had nothing to offer him. Nothing to add to his family's fortune. *Why else would the man still be single?* On the other hand, Barbara may not have come from millionaires, but her parents had enough money to pay for her to attend private school and make sure she graduated from one of the best liberal arts colleges in Memphis.

There may not have been a *coming out* party in her background, but she would fit into his world a hell of a lot better than Darling. She closed her eyes and replayed the last few weeks, his face a constant image in her mind. Jaxon Slater was attractive and rich, not like that bastard Rodney, but she could barely get a moment of his time. He preferred she follow protocol and speak with Darling, who would then speak with Rodney, who would then speak with him. The protocol of hierarchy. Whatever. She hadn't seen Darling follow that protocol. Instead, she just walked in and out of Jaxon's office whenever she wanted to.

The more she thought of him, the more her body ached with anticipation, instead of nearly vomiting at the thought of him as she did with Rodney. One day, she would know Jaxon's touch. As the image of him grew stronger in her mind, her hand slid down her body, doing the things she imagined he would do one day. The feel of her fingers at her core excited her. When the moan left her lips, she flipped over to get a better position and saw an image of herself in the dresser mirror. Damn! This is what she'd been reduced to, getting off by herself, and all because of Darling.

I'll get her for this!

"Barbara, do you have the final numbers for your budget?" Darling asked, again.

The woman had zoned out, or simply ignored her. It didn't matter because the affect was the same. Everyone in the meeting focused on Barbara, instead of the work that needed to be done.

"I emailed the report to you, yesterday." The woman's lips barely moved.

Even though barely audible, Barbara's words were still a lie.

"I don't have it," Darling replied.

No matter how many times she'd asked Barbara for her numbers over the past several days, there'd always been an excuse. She was sick to death of the other woman and her obvious tactics to sabotage everything. The changes she'd talked Mr. Slater into would benefit everyone, including Barbara.

"I need to pull this together for Mr. Slater," Darling

reminded Barbara. "Please go print off a hard copy and bring it back to the meeting?"

"I don't—"

"What?" Darling leaned forward in her chair and rested her arms on the table in front of her. "They're completed, right?" She waited for Barbara to admit to everyone that she'd been lying. At this point, Darling could use it as a reason to fire her. She didn't need a headache with every request she made.

"Yes, but—?" Wide-eyed, Barbara scanned the room as if searching for someone to jump in and back her up.

"Then, we'll wait for you to bring the spreadsheets back to the meeting, so that we can review them and continue." She had penned in some projections for Barbara's numbers, but the actual projections were still needed. She didn't want to fall flat on her face when she presented the final numbers to Jaxon She didn't want him to think she expected any *special* concessions.

Barbara returned within moments, reinforcing Darling's conviction that Barbara had the freaking work completed. The damn woman just wanted to be difficult and ignore Darling's authority.

"Here they are." Barbara slapped the documents on the edge of the conference room table and sat.

Darling stared at the pages resting on the table beside Barbara. "Do you want to read those aloud, or do you want to allow everyone to have a copy to review?"

Barbara slid the report over to Kathy who passed them on to Darling.

After glancing at them, Darling handed them to back to Kathy—her assistant. "Could you please make a set of copies for everyone here?"

"Sure." Kathy hurried from the room.

"It looks like my projections for Barbara's group were pretty accurate," she told everyone. "Mr. Slater approved my plan as long as the numbers matched the proposal. He has given us permission to plus up quite a bit for the end of the year. That means a lot more travel for everyone."

Some team members smiled, while others waited. Maybe because they wanted to know about the part she hadn't shared. The part she'd hoped would get the last remaining hold-outs on *team Barbara* to switch teams.

"How does the timeline work for the people with families who didn't travel before you took over?" Barbara interjected.

Perfect!

"Because of the increased travel, I've asked Mr. Slater to take another look at everyone's compensation plans. As a result of that and added responsibilities, he's in agreement with me that everyone should receive adjusted compensation and benefits, including increases in paid time off."

"Darling, that's fantastic!" Kathy said as she entered the room.

"Human resources will be contacting everyone regarding the changes," Darling continued. "And they will be immediate."

"That's not possible," Barbara said with a nasty edge to her voice.

Why? Because I got something done that you couldn't? "What do you mean?" Darling asked.

"Rodney told me that there wasn't enough money in the budget when I went to him for my team last year."

That's because Rodney didn't listen to you; he screwed you. "I know, but there have been some changes since then. Because of the added responsibilities that we'll all be taking on, it's the only thing that made sense to me, Rodney and Mr. Slater."

Barbara sat up in her seat and for once, paid attention to the numbers displayed on the presentation in front of her. "But how can you—I wasn't able to—"

"We've been working on the changes since the announcement was first made. It's the only way," Darling continued as she scanned the room. "We feel comfortable asking you guys to take on the additional obligations."

Various voices around the room, including the few huddled around Barbara spoke, "Thanks, Darling."

Darling knew the additional money would win over a few of Barbara's loyal team members, but she still had to figure out what to do about the woman herself. She wasn't going to make anything easy.

Darling was determined not to lie down and let Barbara take this away from her. The politics between Rodney and Barbara and the humdrum of the call center didn't excite her. But, with the role changes, it was worth the fight. She could get her life back on track. Move out of her parents' house with or without money from Steve.

"Steve, I don't care what you do." Darling paused. "I just want my share of everything. How I get it doesn't matter."

She did not need this on top of everything at work. She didn't want to have another annoying unproductive conversation with her soon-to-be ex. He never had anything positive to say and she always felt like crap when she hung up the phone.

"All I'm saying," he said, "is that instead of us selling the house, my future wife wants it."

"Your *future* wife!" Why would she give a damn about what his *future* wife wanted? "You didn't care about anything when we were together. I begged you for everything you're asking me to help you give to her." She thought about the struggle she had dragging him out to look at houses. She and the realtor viewed half of them without him. He'd flown out of town minutes after closing, and she'd spent the first night in their new home alone.

"I—I—"

"Never mind, I don't care. I get it." She gave the

bastard everything, but he gave her nothing, and now, he wanted what was left. But, this time, he wanted her to give it to him, so that he could give it to his future wife. It made her want to scream!

"We like the schools in the area. And when the baby is older—"

Baby? What the hell! She'd wanted children. His children.

She didn't want to hear any more about anything. "I don't care. I don't need to know the details." She already had her answers. He liked magazine covers, and she'd been traded in for the latest one. She'd made the mistake of falling in love. He didn't. She wanted to slam her cell against the wall. "Just have your lawyer contact mine. I've got to go."

No matter how many long deep breaths she took, nothing worked to take the edge off her anger. Like a caged animal in a zoo, Darling circled her room over and over replaying Steve's words in her head. All the things she'd wanted with him, he was willingly giving to someone else. All the years they'd been together hadn't meant a damn thing to him! She walked to the bathroom to run a bath. The closed door signaled that one of her parents was in it, and she didn't want to wait. Doubling back to her room, she grabbed her purse and headed out the front door.

The longer she drove, the more the street signs and headlights of oncoming cars blurred. Only when the dampness of her shirt began to send a chill through her did she realize she'd been crying the entire time.

Where she was headed might be the biggest mistake of her life, but it was the only place she wanted to be, and *he* was the only person she wanted to be with. She pulled into the crescent shaped drive and opened the driver's side door. At the request of the valet, she handed him her keys.

"Ma'am are you okay?" asked the valet.

"Yes, thank you." She dabbed at her eyes with her palm. "Allergies." She walked through the revolving doors shivering a little as the cold air hit her wet shirt. Her sneakers squeaked across the marble floors. She didn't stop 'til she reached the elevators.

Jaxon opened his hotel door, and thought he'd fallen asleep reading through budget proposals, conjuring up an image of a naked, smiling Darling. Except she wasn't naked and she definitely wasn't smiling.

She just stood there, silently with the tracks of her dried tears noticeable on her beautiful chocolate skin.

He reached for her. "Are you okay?" he asked.

She turned to walk away. "I'm sorry. I don't know what I'm doing here."

He grabbed her, tugging her backwards against his body and wrapped his arms tighter around her. Her round butt met his groin and he became very aware of her body's softness and his desire. He spoke into the ponytail she wore, "Don't leave." He paused. "Come in."

The breath she released slowly, relaxed her into his body. The warmth of her against him erased the small amount of control he held onto. Out of respect for her tears, he pulled his body away from hers because it for damn sure, wasn't listening to him.

Darling turned to face him. "I apologize for showing up here like this. I just didn't know where else to go."

He pulled her into the hotel room and locked the door behind her. "Darling, you're always welcomed wherever I am." He motioned toward a chair. "Sit and tell me what's going on." He grabbed a bottle of wine and two glasses. "Would you like a drink?"

When she nodded yes, he filled both and handed her one.

She took a long sip before she spoke, "My ex called. He's marrying the woman he left me for and she's pregnant." She kicked off her sneakers and curled her jean clad legs up underneath her. "And they want to live in the house he and I bought and renovated." Her body deflated with her explanation.

"I've never been married." He swirled his glass of wine. "I don't think I've ever wanted to take the chance on falling out of love," he mumbled. His shock at admitting that to her and to himself, made him throw back what was left in his glass.

Glistening eyes looked up at him. "What do you mean?"

"Falling in love is always fun, but when it's over— that's the hard part. Moving on." He'd watched his father move on, while his mother sat waiting. She'd been stuck for the longest time with only him, Jaxon, to give all her love to and he didn't deserve it any more than his father.

"You say that as if you understand, yet you say you haven't been in love. If that's true, how do you know so much about it?"

He leaned against the wall where he stood, and fisted his hands in his pockets. "My father left my mother for a stewardess." He chuckled at the cliché of his life. Rich man leaving family for arm candy, too typical.

"I don't know what to say," she said in a soft voice.

He loved the sound of her voice. When it needed to be firm and strong, during department meetings, it was. When it needed to be gentle and encouraging, while they made love, it was. He was beginning to think he'd do anything to hear the latter again.

"There's nothing for you to say." He pushed away from the wall and refilled his wine glass, and then took a sip. "As a kid, I heard my mother cry herself to sleep and watched her go out on dates with anyone, so that she wouldn't be alone. It was enough to convince me that being alone made better sense."

"So, you never wanted to fall in love?"

"No." He didn't think he did, but not even he could explain why he was still in Memphis. "I avoided it."

"I agree with you."

"Don't agree with me." He didn't want to agree with himself. He wanted her to love, and maybe—to love him.

"Why not? Steve and I were together forever. All I thought about was marriage and *his* children from the moment I met him."

The fact that she wasn't married and didn't have another man's kids made him happy. "Maybe he wasn't the right person."

"Now, you sound like my friend, Annette, and my mother." She smiled, weakly.

"You should listen to us." He grabbed the television remote and searched for something funny. Something to put a smile on her face. "You need to laugh and drink more wine. Relax."

And stay with me tonight.

"I don't think that's a good idea." She rose from the chair. "I should leave. I have to work in the morning."

"Sit down." He grinned. "I give you permission to come in late." His smile widened. "What do you feel like watching?"

###

Darling woke reluctantly the next morning, not because of the piercing whistles of the train—which strangely seemed to be absent—but because it was hard to ignore the light shining on her face. Crap, she squeezed her eyes tighter to try to keep out the warm glow. The odd morning quiet and the softness of the sheets around her made her relax deeper into the bed's mattress. As she nestled she bumped—

Her eyes popped open.

Oh, my God! She'd fallen asleep in Jaxon's hotel room. With her eyes and her hands, she scanned her body. Thank God, she was still dressed and she didn't remember having sex. That was definite because there was no way she'd ever forget one touch from Jaxon.

Beside her, Jaxon slept on top of the covers that she'd only moments ago snuggled beneath. His bare muscled chest tempted her to lean over and kiss her way down to his navel. Maybe follow that little fine line of black hair that disappeared beneath the waist of his pants.

When she attempted to ease herself from the bed, his hand reached out and grabbed her arm. "Don't leave," he whispered.

The heavily accented voice that made her stay in B.B. King's, take that carriage ride and spend the night with him rolled over her awakening her body in many ways. "We both have to go to work," she said without conviction. "And this would be a huge mistake."

His beautiful green eyes stared at her. "Why would this be a mistake?"

The desire grew within her to stay where she was. But, what sense would it make to give in to it. "Because I'm still falling out of love," she explained, "and you're scared of love."

"Not because I own the company?"

She ran her fingers through his hair smoothing out small twists and tangles. "That's only part of it. You don't really know me."

"I know enough." His grip on her arm loosened as he rose to his forearms and linked his fingers with hers.

"Do you?" She studied his beautiful face. "Do you really?" He didn't know anything about her, aside from the fact that she was divorcing a jerk. Would he still want her if he knew that what he saw of her were remnants of the life she'd had with Steve, not her reality, now.

She untwined her fingers from his and slipped from the bed. She had full intentions of leaving no room for a romance.

CHAPTER NINE

Darling sat in the parking lot of Slater Enterprises and listened to the morning DJ joke with callers on the radio. She surveyed her outfit again. Would anyone notice that the shirt she wore belonged to Jaxon? Actually, it had been one of her favorites—on him. The green fabric didn't do as much for her dark skin and brown eyes as it had for him. She slid her fingers along the soft cotton remembering the intensity of his gaze as he silently watched her dress.

Thank goodness, she'd had a skirt pegged for the cleaners in the trunk of her car.

His request of, *"Don't leave,"* replayed in her head as if someone had stuck a CD on repeat.

The simple words broke her heart because she hadn't wanted to go. But they were both kidding themselves if they thought they could be anything other than what they were.

The fingers of her hand tangled in the frayed threads of the lining of her purse as she searched for her lipstick.

Angling the bag toward the sunlight, she peered through the hole at the tube of lipstick mocking her. Didn't that sum up her whole crazy life! Everything looked pretty on the outside, but if you looked closer, there were holes everywhere.

Jaxon's father had willed him a business worth millions. Her father, one of the most intelligent men she knew, didn't even graduate from high school. What on earth would their relationship look like? Pathetically, she admitted to herself, this wasn't the first time she and her family were not good enough for something.

Or someone.

Aside from the wedding, Steve and his family hadn't interacted with hers. Damn it, Steve didn't come from money, but he was in love with it and everything it gave him. He limited contact with not only her family but his own. None of them fit with the future he had planned. His picture-perfect family included: a wife who could grace the covers of Essence or Vogue and two perfect kids. Kids, who would attend the right schools and eventually, get the right jobs and marry the right people.

Perfect! Just Perfect.

Maybe all of this was payback. Maybe she deserved it for allowing herself to turn her back on her family.

What would Jaxon's mother think of her family? Of her?

She grabbed the collar of the shirt she wore and brought it to her nose. The scent of him flooded her. But, she knew that was her imagination hard at work because the shirt had hung in the closet in its plastic from the cleaners, freshly laundered.

The pen in Barbara's hand slipped to the floor. That green shirt she would recognize anywhere, because she'd had too many dreams of ripping it from Jaxon's body and waking up wearing it the next morning herself. But, this wasn't a dream and she wasn't the one wearing it. "Hello, Darling." She tried to make her voice sound normal. *Did you have fun last night?* "I got Kathy's message to run the meeting until you arrived."

"Thank you." Darling walked to the front of the small conference room and stood beside Barbara. "What have you guys reviewed so far? Any questions about anything?"

No. They don't have any questions, but I do. Where did you sleep last night?

"Kathy emailed me your presentation and I followed it pretty closely." Now, Barbara knew why she couldn't get a moment of Jaxon's time. Because he was busy screwing her! Ms. High and Mighty wasn't so different from her after all. "Will Mr. Slater also be joining us, today?"

"Mr. Slater?" she asked a little too innocently.

"Yes." Barbara marveled at how stupid Darling must think she and everybody else was. *If you don't want people asking questions, don't show up wearing your boss' clothes.* "When I couldn't find you earlier, I went to check with Mr. Slater, but he wasn't in."

"Oh, okay." Darling's hands slid down her sides smoothing wrinkles that didn't exist from her shirt. "Rodney probably could've answered your questions, too."

"He did, but what about Mr. Slater?" If she asked the question enough, maybe the rest of the idiots in the room would understand too.

"I don't think he'll be joining us." She waved an arm at the presentation on the screen. "This is pretty basic. It doesn't need any input from him." She paused. "But, if you have any questions about anything, let me know. If I can't answer it, Rodney or Mr. Slater would be more than willing to help."

"I guess you're right." Barbara ground her teeth. "It's all pretty basic."

The new girl really thought she could beat her by sleeping with the boss. Barbara had invested too much time and too many years of her life in Slater Enterprises. She wasn't about to allow some broke chick from the hood to ace her out of the opportunity to get with the man who could once and for all change everything. She'd never have to think about sleeping with someone like Rodney again. She would be able to travel, eat in the best restaurants, and join the best country clubs or whatever she wanted. She had to switch places with Darling and find her way into Jaxon's bed.

Jaxon was standing outside the conference room with Rodney, when he heard someone mention his name. As he listened, Rodney's face reddened a little more each time Barbara said Jaxon's name. He'd planned to sit in on the briefing, not because Darling needed his help, but because he wanted to see her. His shirt on her body turned him on more than he'd thought possible. The only thing easing the ache, which had grown hotter inside of him with every day he'd spent in Memphis, was thinking about taking that shirt off her. In his mind, he pictured himself slowly unfastening each button to tease himself with what he knew was underneath before he peeled the shirt and everything else she wore away from her body.

Darling had slept silently most of the night. At one point, he thought she cried at a dream, but then she smiled. There was no way he'd been able to sleep with her beside him. He knew she would leave as soon as she woke.

Tired as hell, he rested against the nearby wall and continued to listen to the women inside. "Rodney, what is that damn Barbara up to, now?"

Rodney offered him a whispered response, "Sir, I don't know."

Jaxon knew he should've listened to his gut and made Barbara take the package he'd threatened her with when they consolidated the groups. But, Rodney had pleaded for her. The entire situation was his fault! The relationship between her and Rodney jeopardized everything. One wrong move and the affair would become grounds for a sexual harassment lawsuit. The fact she hadn't threatened it already surprised him.

"I thought you said she'd calm down. That you had this under control?"

"I thought—" Rodney contorted his body to peer around Jaxon and into the conference room.

"Did you imply to Barbara that there was something between Darling and myself? Jaxon demanded. "Or, that you were going to try to change Barbara's or Darling's status within the company?"

Rodney's attention snapped back to Jaxon. His already flushed face glistened at the temples. "No—no, sir."

"Then why is she always so hostile toward Darling?" The longer he looked at him the more the damn idiot irritated him. Jaxon had never wanted to run the company, but he wasn't going to let a little weasel like Rodney be the reason the business failed. Competition was one thing. Incompetence was something different.

"I don't know." Rodney swallowed hard. But I can find out."

"No, I don't want you to do anything." Jaxon paused. "I think you've done enough to put this company in a bad situation."

"Sir, I—?"

Jaxon couldn't remember a time when he'd ever seen a man near tears. But, Rodney's eyes glistened and if they stood there any longer, he was sure the man would break down, sobbing.

He didn't want to see a grown man cry.

Jaxon began to walk away. "In fact," he said over his shoulder. "I think this would be a great time for you to take a little time off. Go on a vacation with your family for a few weeks."

Rodney slumped against the wall. "Sir—?"

"Vacation, Rodney, vacation." He turned and walked to his office.

At his desk, Jaxon poured over paperwork. With Rodney out of the office for a few weeks, he'd have a real reason to be in town. But, that wouldn't solve his problems with Barbara or stop his desire for—

The scent of her lotion announced her. After she'd dressed to leave, he'd spent a few moments before he stepped into the shower just standing in the hotel bathroom letting the lavender of the lotion and the soap wash over him. He'd never paid any kind of attention to the toiletries lining the hotel sink. But, now he couldn't get their smell out of his head. There was no way for him to ever forget their nights together or that scent.

"Excuse me, Mr. Slater."

He looked up to see her standing in the doorway. Her voice reminded him of the softness of her words when she'd forced them both to leave for work. He'd wanted her to say screw it all and let's spend the day together.

"Jaxon," he reminded her.

"May I come in?" she asked.

"Of course." He hated the formality between them, even though he knew it was appropriate.

She closed the door behind her. "Mr. Slater, last night was a huge mistake."

She tugged at the shirt that looked better on her than on him. It hugged her breasts in a way that it never fit his chest.

"And I think it's already been noticed," she continued.

"By Barbara?"

She frowned, accenting the distressed look in her eyes. "Yes. How'd you know?"

"Rodney and I were outside of the conference room earlier."

"Then you understand what I'm saying is what's best."

Damn. Nothing could ever just be easy. "No." He smiled. "But I'll do what you want."

"It's just that she's digging and if she keeps digging…" Her eyes closed and she rubbed her hand along the bridge of her nose. "I don't want her undercutting my authority. Or yours."

He knew he needed to give careful consideration to everything. But, the more time he spent with her, the more he wanted to be with her. Giving her what she wanted was beginning to deny him what he wanted. "Even if she keeps it up, she won't find anything because there isn't anything. Right?" He waited.

She nodded her head in agreement.

"And as far as your authority, she'll have no choice but to work with you for the short-term."

Some of the worry drained from her expression, but was replaced with curiosity. "Why?"

"I've sent Rodney on an extended vacation." He paused. "Barbara, will never work with you if she can keep running to him. Rodney's been with this company for a long time, but he's risking everything with his behavior."

She quirked an eyebrow at him.

"Hypocritical. I know. But, unlike Rodney and Barbara, I'm not making empty promises to you or interfering with anything you try to do." No, he hadn't promised her anything, but staring at her leaning against that door as if she wasn't certain the lock worked created a strange desire to promise her everything.

"No, you just gave me a whole department."

"That was Rodney's decision, not mine. But, I did approve it." Anger jolted through him with his next thought. "I think he had plans to replace Barbara with you…in his bed."

She pulled away from the door behind her and took a step toward him. But, something made her stop. "I would never—"

He waved off her response. As thankful as he was for her confirmation, he didn't want to think of her in another man's bed. "I know. But, I don't think he did."

"Is Rodney leaving for vacation because of me?"

Jaxon leaned back in his desk chair as his anger at Rodney's intentions toward Darling subsided. "I believe his interference will make this transition harder."

"I don't know." She paused. "What about you and your company? I don't want to be the cause of—"

He'd heard her mention his authority the first time, but it pleased him to hear her ask the question again. She wasn't just worried about herself. "So, you do care." He smiled.

"I'm serious," she responded.

"Me, too." He wanted to get up and hold her to reassure her that everything would be okay. Besides, the way she pressed her back against that door, again, she would never allow him to touch her. Not here.

"I just really think," she lowered her voice, "we need to be discreet."

"What does that mean?" He knew he must've interpreted her wrong. "Are you agreeing to dinner, or a proper return of my shirt?" There was not anything proper about how he wanted the shirt returned.

The smile that slid across her face was meant to entice him, and it did. "Jaxon be serious." She turned to leave, but paused and looked over her shoulder. "I'll return the shirt after I have it dry-cleaned."

His office was large. Big enough to carve into two smaller ones. But, he'd insisted that his desk be placed along the huge window opposite his office door. During particularly sunny days, it was a pain. But, as he watched Darling stroll down the hallway, he was thankful. The perfect view. The sway of her hips threw his imagination into hyper-drive. The tightening of his pants pinched at his groin. He reached beneath his desk to shift the weight and hopefully, find a little relief. A voice startled him and he straightened, quickly.

"Mr. Slater, may I come in?" She waited just on the other side of the door's threshold.

"Barbara," he acknowledged her, and then glanced at the files on his desk. "I really need to finish reviewing these."

"It won't take long," she said.

There was no way she'd missed Darling strolling out of his office and she'd probably watched him as he'd ogled Darling's ass. The woman was smart, or she wouldn't have picked such an easy target like Rodney. "Come in."

She reached for the door to close it.

"Please leave it open." All he needed was for her to be able to point to any time they spent alone to indicate him in any future lawsuits she may have planned.

She frowned at the statement, but pushed the door back open. "Sir, Rodney just informed me that he's leaving for vacation."

"Yes for a few weeks. A little rest and relaxation with his wife."

Her back straightened a little at the mention of Rodney's wife. "If I have a concern about my department, am I allowed to escalate it to your attention?"

"Again, I'd prefer you take it through Darling."

A quick twitch of her mouth indicated her annoyance at the mention of Darling's name. "But, what if my concern is her?"

"Do you have an issue?" He leaned back into the leather of his oversized desk chair.

"No, not really, but what if I did?"

"Barbara, if an issue of that sort arises while Rodney is out, you can bring it to my attention."

"Thank you." Smiling she turned to leave. "Thank you so much."

CHAPTER TEN

"Excuse me." The words were accompanied by a tap on Darling's shoulder.

Darling turned to stare into the green eyes of a well-coiffed older woman who stood just a few inches taller than her.

"I've been wandering around lost." She smiled. "It's been so long since I've been here. Can you help me find Jaxon Slater's office?

"Yes, ma'am." Darling glanced down the hallway in front of her. "I'm headed that way myself. I can walk with you."

"Great." The woman extended a hand. "I'm Elaine Slater."

Darling nearly passed out. *Jaxon's mother?*

She was perfectly groomed from her stylishly tailored skirt suit to her flawless silver hair. Not one strand out of place.

"It's a pleasure to meet you. I'm Darling Crawford."

"Darling. Oh, yes. I've heard a lot about you." She

grinned warmly. "My son thinks very highly of you."

The fact that Jaxon and his mom had discussed her filled her with something. A feeling that surprised her, but she welcomed it. The feeling of joy. "I hope they were all good things." Something inside of her nagged because she wanted to ask more details but instead, she smiled at the compliment.

The woman's reassuring smile pleased Darling.

"All great things," his mother said.

Darling knocked lightly on Jaxon's door. At his response, she pushed it open and walked in after his mother.

"Surprise, honey," his mother said.

"Mom." A warm smile lit up his face. He came around his desk and met her at the door with a big bear hug.

The man that Darling had come to know vanished. For once, there were no barriers as she watched him take his mother's hand and lead her to a nearby chair. Before his mother asked, he pulled a bottle of water from his office fridge and poured half into a cup then placed the bottle on the table beside her.

"What are you doing here?" he asked, taking the chair next to her. "Why didn't you call? I could've met you at the airport."

The barrage of questions ended when his mother threw up a hand to halt them. "That's why I said surprise." Warm genuine laughter bubbled through her whole body.

He scanned the space around her. "Where are your bags?"

"Melanie picked me up." She drank from the glass he'd placed beside her. "We thought we could treat you to lunch."

Briefly, his eyes darted to Darling. "Mom—"

"Knock, knock," said one of the most beautiful statuesque blondes Darling had ever seen in her life. If she hadn't graced Vogue in the past, they'd missed the opportunity to sell millions of copies to drooling college frat boys and impressionable girls who would want to look just like her.

The guarded Jaxon that Darling knew from meetings and office luncheons reappeared. Darling wandered if anyone else noticed. Or, maybe she saw what she wanted to see. Darling stood as tall as her stubby legs would allow and let her right hand slide down the length of her consignment store black skirt. The feel of the fabric was cheap beneath her touch, she knew it would not compare to the suit the model wore. The fit could only have been achieved by the hands of a master tailor. Definitely not off the rack, and no way it came from a *previously worn* rack. Darling wanted to turn and bolt from the room.

"Melanie, come in." Jaxon shook her hand. "It's good to see you again." He nodded at Darling. "This is my Director of Meeting Planning and Events, Darling Crawford." The smile he offered the beautiful woman was warm, friendly.

Although it didn't compare to the smile offered Darling when she'd dressed at his hotel room the other day, it still angered her. Melanie didn't have to hide how she felt or what she wanted from Jaxon. All Darling could do was hide what she wanted because she couldn't give him what *Melanie* could give him. Melanie would fit better in his future than she ever would. And from the smile on his mother's face, Melanie was who she wanted for him, too.

She'd never accept me.

"Thank you." She smiled at him, and then at Darling. "It's good to see you, too." She glanced between Darling and Jaxon. "Are we interrupting anything?" Melanie waited patiently for someone to respond.

Darling felt as if everyone in the room expected her to answer. "No," Darling said at last. "I needed to give Mr. Slater these reports." She sat the files she'd been clutching against her chest on the table. "But, we can review them later."

"Great," his mother said. "We made reservations for

the restaurant I love at The Peabody."

Jaxon rested his hand on top of the pile of reports Darling had placed on the table. "Ladies, I have so much to finish."

The office began to feel a little small. Darling didn't think she belonged in the room with the model and the millionaires. She began to take a few steps backwards toward the door. "Don't worry about the reports Mr. Slater. We can look at everything later."

The closer Darling moved toward the door, the more Jaxon closed the distance between them. Only inches away from her, he paused and glanced at the other women in the room before focusing on her. "Are you sure?" He paused. "Can you handle this without me?"

"Definitely." She nodded at his mother and the model. "Please go."

Now.

Yes, now before her head exploded from pretending to be okay with sending Jaxon off with a woman she couldn't compete against in any way.

"Thank you, Darling," his mom interjected. "Then, it's settled." She stood and pulled a little at the hem of her skirt. "Let's go and enjoy ourselves."

Arm and arm with his mother, Jaxon and Melanie disappeared around the corner out of her sight. God, she wanted to cry, but there wasn't any reason. He was doing exactly what he should be doing.

Barbara popped up as she walked out of the office. "That was a beautiful woman. She's probably Memphis royalty. You know...the best education and old money." The smile she flashed was too big. The heifer was happy to see Jaxon with another woman.

Barbara never failed to know exactly how to make her feel like crap. "It's really none of my business," Darling replied.

"Sure, it is." She turned to walk away. "Can't have Mr. Slater splitting his time and *interests*."

She swore she heard the tramp laugh as she walked away.

###

Jaxon sat across the table from his well-intentioned mother and Melanie surrounded by the historic beauty of The Peabody, but his mind was miles away. The moment Melanie walked into his office…Darling had tried to make herself disappear. He needed to see her and let her know that everything would be okay. *Shit*. What was he thinking? He didn't have anything to apologize for. She'd told him to go, and no matter how much he pushed, she refused to act on what she felt. He didn't even know what he wanted to do himself.

As he sat across from the beautiful woman, he had to admit her attractiveness would intimidate most women and men. With the platforms she wore, she stood shoulder to shoulder with him and her hair held the perfect shades of honey and wheat. And, even in a suit, her body was hard for a man to resist. But, Darling, all five feet of her turned him on more than any woman he'd ever met, including this one.

"Jaxon, how much longer do you think you'll be in town?" Melanie asked.

As long as it takes, to determine what was happening with Darling, him, and his company. "Maybe a month."

She smiled and with a toss of her head flipped her golden hair over her shoulder. "That's great. We'll have plenty of time to explore." She smiled. "Memphis, that is."

"I don't know how much free time I'll have." He pushed away from the prime rib sandwich in front of him and leaned back in his seat. "One of my senior directors is taking a little time off." That was true enough.

"Oh, why?" asked his mother. She removed the tomato from her sandwich and placed it on the side of her plate.

He'd seen her do that same thing a million times

before. "Mom, why don't you send it back?"

She smiled. "There's no reason to cause anyone any extra trouble when I can simply pull it off myself."

Jaxon couldn't help but smile. His mother never complained about anything. He got back to his mother's earlier question. "My senior director has a lot of personal business to take care of. A little time off will do him good."

"Well, hopefully, the young lady, Darling, will be able to help you keep everything going," his mother said.

"I think so." He thought for a second. "A lot of work needs to be done."

"How long has she been working with you?" Melanie asked between bites of grilled eggplant.

"Not very long. My senior director hired her. She has a lot of experience, and we both think she'll be able to help us revamp our meetings program."

Melanie stopped eating. "You seem to have a lot of confidence in her."

He had more than confidence in her. He was falling in love with her. "Yes."

Dinner had been painless enough, but his mother never gave up that easily. If she thought she had a "good" woman for him, she kept insisting. For every memorable night he'd had, there'd been almost as many disasters. "Mom, I don't think Melanie and I are right for each other."

They'd walked Melanie to the exit and waited with her while the valet returned with her car. He'd convinced his mother to have a cocktail in the lobby before heading to their rooms. Sitting beneath the iconic chandeliers of The Peabody, Jaxon remembered past visits he and his mother had made. The times they'd stood at the historic fountain watching the famous ducks walk down the red carpet and climb into the water. The brunches they'd shared. He couldn't figure out how the years had passed so quickly.

As his mother sat sipping from her wine glass, he noticed her hair was a little more silver, and there were a few more fine lines gracing her forehead.

What would he do with the rest of his life? Who would he spend those years with? Would he ever give her the grandchildren she wanted?

"Son, you haven't even given her a chance," she said with an edge of concern to her voice.

There was no reason to go into detail about the impossible situation between him and Darling. "Please. I promise you I can handle my own love life."

"Can you?" She stretched out her legs and relaxed into the oversized leather chair. "If I wait on you to find someone, I'll never have any grandchildren."

He put his cocktail on the table next to him. Sliding forward in his chair, he stared into his mother's worried eyes. There was so much to share with her, but first, he needed her to know. "Mom, I don't know what kind of father I would be—"

"Son, you would be a great father because you're a great man." Her eyes glistened. "I was afraid you would feel this way. I didn't want you to doubt yourself because of us."

"I know, but you can't pick my wife for me because you want grandkids."

"Of course, I want grandkids. I'm not trying to—I don't want you to never know what it's like to feel the love and happiness that grows in my heart every time I look into your eyes."

He reached across the small table, and placed his hand on top of hers. "Mom, I've been thinking a lot about a family, lately."

The sadness in her eyes drained away.

"But, you have to let me do this my own way."

Silently, his mother stared for a long while. "You've

found someone. Well, tell me who is she?" She leaned forward and covered his hand with her other. "Do I know her family?"

"No, you don't know her family." Hell, he didn't know her family. "It's complicated."

"Complicated? How?" The frown lines etched in her forehead deepened.

No matter his age, she would never stop worrying about him. "It's nothing you can help me with. I have to do it myself."

"Well, if that Darling doesn't know how you feel...it's her loss." She released his hand and leaned back into her chair.

He blinked in response to his mother's words and knowledge. "What? How did you know?" Since his childhood, she'd always been able to tell him what he was thinking before he knew. She knew who he was attracted to in high school, or which of his friends he was fighting with. And it didn't change in college. She had mom radar that never allowed him to hide.

"Son, I know you." She laughed warmly. "I knew there had to be some reason you weren't trying to leave Memphis. The minute Melanie entered your office you changed and so did Darling."

He wanted to deny it, but it was nice to talk about it with someone. "I don't know what to do." That was the problem in a nutshell.

"Have you told her?" His mother lifted her glass of wine to her nose, and inhaled the bouquet.

"No." He sighed and fell back against his chair. "When we first met, she didn't work for us. Then she disappeared for a few months. And then there's Rodney and Barbara." The more he listened to himself, the more he understood why Darling pulled away at every opportunity. If he didn't know what he wanted, why should she trust him?

She nodded. "So, the job is the problem?"

"It's complicated. She's going through a nasty divorce."

"No, son, it's not complicated at all." She sipped her cocktail. "When your father left, life changed. But, like an idiot, I kept waiting. For some reason, I thought he might come back. I wanted the nightmare to end, but it didn't. Then, one day, you were a man—no longer a boy, and I was old and alone."

His mother's words cut right through him. He'd always known of her pain, but she'd never voiced it. "Mom—"

"No, it's okay. The reason, I'm telling you this is because I know the way I lived my life affected the way you live yours. That's why I play matchmaker." She laughed. "I guess I'm trying to make up for all those years of nothing."

There it was. His mother blamed herself for his fucked up life, but that wasn't on her. It wasn't even on his father. It was on him. He'd checked out a long time ago and until he met Darling, he hadn't cared. Sex without strings had kept his head on straight and his heart his own. "Mom, you were dealing with your own pain."

"Yes, but I never should've stopped being a mother to my son."

He leaned over and kissed her on the cheek. "You didn't."

She patted his hand closest to her with her own. "Yes, I did. But, I promise, I won't ever do it again."

He knew his mother wouldn't break a promise she made to him. But, nothing she'd done had scarred him. It was his own fear of hurting a woman the way his father had her, as well as, the slim chance that someone might hurt him. "I don't know what to do, but I can't stop thinking about her."

"Son, a divorce can be difficult for a woman. People who've never been through it can't really understand what I mean. Right now, aside from a broken heart, she's letting go of the dream she had with her ex-husband. Family. Children. Whatever her dream was." His mother's gaze drifted off into the distance before she refocused on him.

"She probably doesn't trust men and isn't sure if it's worth it to go through it all again."

"I know she cares for me, but she's scared." He closed his eyes and listened to the pianist. The soloist's soft sad music bounced through the empty halls of The Peabody. "What if I can't be a good man to her?" If he could confess his fears to his mother and to himself, maybe he could proclaim his feelings to Darling.

"I was scared. I didn't want to feel *that* way again, ever. As a mom, I didn't want anyone to hurt my son. What if you would've lost not only your father, but a step-father? I couldn't do it." She paused. "Can you be her friend and expect nothing?"

He searched his heart and ignored the argument his body put up in disagreement. "I want to be whatever she needs. Whatever she'll allow me to be."

"All those years ago, I needed a friend. Too many men wanted money..." She cleared her throat. "...Companionship, but no one wanted a no-strings-attached friendship."

"Be her friend?" he asked. How was he supposed to be only a friend to a beautiful sexy woman that filled his dreams every night?

"Listen to her. Be there for her. Don't try to be her hero or her prince charming. Why do men always think a woman needs rescuing?" she asked rhetorically. "You don't know what this other man did to her, or what her dreams with him were. Let her know how wonderful a man you are." She smiled. "Show her the man I know and she'll love you as much as I do."

CHAPTER ELEVEN

Barbara had wasted too many weekends reviewing reports for upcoming tradeshows at Slater Enterprises watching Jaxon and waiting on the perfect opportunity. The bang of the overloaded box to the thinly carpeted floor ricocheted through the empty hallways. A happy tingle shot threw her as she dragged the box stuffed with brochures and useless trinkets.

Jaxon rounded the corner and rushed toward her. As he neared, shock or confusion clouded his expression. He slowed his approach. "Barbara, what are you doing here on a weekend?" he asked as he assisted her with the load she dragged.

She marveled at how easily he lifted the box and stacked it on top of another case lined up against a nearby wall.

"I needed to ship out a few more things for the tradeshow next week." The simplicity of her plan pleased her. She stifled a smile. "Instead of shipping all these." She waved her arm in the direction of the various boxes she'd filled and labeled. "I can drop some off with Darling."

"Does she need to carry it with her?"

No, but there's no other way to get him to Darling's house. She hadn't seen the woman who'd visited with his mother in weeks, so maybe there was still a chance for her. And when he sees Darling's neighborhood and her parents, he'll see she's not the right woman. There's no way she would fit into his life better than her. "She doesn't need the stuff for the booth. But, I pulled together packages of brochures and other items that she can use."

"What would she use them for?"

How many questions will he ask? Rodney would never have questioned her. All she ever needed to do was flash a little skin and lick her lips, and he gave her whatever she wanted. Or, at least, she thought he did. He didn't give her the big ass budget Darling had. Bigger budget meant more shows, more sales, better bonuses, and happier employees. Everyone practically whistled while they worked. She would've been able to do the same thing, if she would've had the same support. "This is the first time we've attended this conference. I don't want to take any chances. With these materials, she can set-up and test the booth. She'll know ahead of time if we need more space or more materials."

He didn't speak, but seemed to mull over her words as he scanned the crap load of boxes strewn through the hallway.

She continued, "Sir, would you mind helping me load my car?" She beamed her most innocent smile.

As they loaded her car, Barbara, rehearsed what she could say to get him to drive to Darlings' house.

"Looks like you're set." He closed her trunk and slapped his hands together to remove the dust of the boxes from them.

Barbara reached for her phone. "Thank you, Mr. Slater." She tapped the screen to wake it up, and pretended to read a text message. "Sir, I'm sorry, but there's an emergency. I have to pick up my nephew. Would it be okay if I call Darling and let her know you'll bring this stuff to her?"

"I have plans. Can't you take it later after you help with your nephew?"

Damn. She thought he might jump at the chance to go to Darling's house. "Sir, she's driving out Monday and she's going to need this stuff." *Not really.* But, by the time he found out the truth, he'd be thankful she'd stopped him from getting any more involved with Darling.

"Okay, text me her address and pop your trunk." He attempted to squelch a smile.

"Thank you. You're a life saver." She hid a smile of her own.

Jaxon had strolled the deserted hallways of Slater Enterprises with no purpose, but no matter which way he turned, he ended his walk in the same place—Darling's office. Because he had no reason to be in Memphis and there was only one woman, he wanted to spend his time with. The weekends were nothing to him but two days that annoyed the hell out of him because he couldn't see her. He knew the ache in his gut wouldn't go away until she returned from her site visit for their next event in Little Rock. The trip to Little Rock would only be for a couple of days, but tell that to the knot in the pit of his stomach. He'd been grateful for the sound of dropping boxes that pulled him down the hall dragging his attention away from her empty chair.

Jaxon relaxed as he drove up to the front of The Peabody. But, he found it difficult to mask his excitement. It became equally as hard for him to wait patiently for his mom to fasten her seatbelt. "Sorry, mom, but this shouldn't take too long. We'll drop off the packages, and then I promise, I'm all yours for the rest of the day."

"It's good to see you smile. Is that because you can't wait to play a game of tennis with me, or because we're stopping by Darling's?" She stared straight ahead, but the subtle smile that curved her lips told Jaxon she understood his motivations too well.

He grinned as he pressed the gas a little too hard, jetting from the curb.

The older neighborhood Jaxon's GPS sent him to could not be correct. Could it? But, as he slowed and reached for the button to ask the navigator to correct his location, he saw her. With her hair pulled high on top of her head neatly into a ponytail, she wore a torso hugging t-shirt and shorts that drew his attention to her round bottom. One shoe on and one off, she ran across the yard chasing behind a little boy with the complexion of butterscotch that held the other one. "Cedric, give that back."

On wobbly legs, the smiling little boy glanced over his shoulder at her, but kept running.

It took a moment to find a parking spot on the crowded two-way street. Jaxon and his mother watched as children and adults climbed out of their cars heading toward Darling. The large front yard had become a temporary playground. A huge inflatable swimming pool had been placed in the center of the yard. Children bubbled with laughter as they splashed and played under the hot Memphis sun. Equally, as many children bounced to the beat of their own giggles, inside a beautiful white castle that rivaled the height of some of the surrounding trees.

An older man plated hot dogs and burgers. A snowy white haired woman whose height and physique resembled Darling's, mingled with the crowd. Each person Darling approached smiled and hugged her as if they'd known her their whole life.

Softly, his mother touched his arm. "Son, should we interrupt?"

"Barbara called to tell her I was coming." He popped the trunk and began to exit the car. "It shouldn't take me long."

She jiggled her seat belt. "I'm coming with you."

Before he could complain, she exited the car.

He grabbed the packages, and approached the crowd. The first day he walked into the corporate offices of Slater Enterprises, he didn't feel as anxious as he did making his way through the crowd toward Darling. Although Barbara had called, he felt that he was intruding on a very private family moment. Work should not cut into her time with the people she loved. How did Barbara manage to talk him into this?

As he passed by the older gentleman on the grill, he was certain that the man was Darling's father. The man's dark skin and facial features mirrored Darlings.

"Well, hello ma'am." Darling's father nodded at Jaxon's mom. "Young man, what can we do for you?"

"Hi, sir, my name is Jaxon Slater and this is my mother, Elaine. We came to drop off a few packages for Darling."

"Darling..." He pointed a long fork in Darling's direction. "...Is over there." He smiled with a slight nod of his head.

Jaxon knew exactly where she stood. He needed no assistance, but he allowed his eyes to follow the fork. "Thank you."

"No problem." Mr. Crawford jabbed at some hot dogs and corn. "Would you like something to eat?"

"No thank you," he said as he walked toward Darling.

His mother lingered behind. "I'd love one of those burgers," his mother said. "No tomato if you wouldn't mind."

As he neared Darling, she let go of the young boy she'd finally caught and glared. "What are you doing here? How did you know where I lived?" She stomped toward him.

The anger of her words froze him where he stood. Lifting the box he carried, he said, "Barbara told me you needed this, and asked me to deliver it." He glanced over his shoulder at his car. "I have more in the trunk of my car."

She attempted to snatch the boxes from his arms. Their weight or his grip deterred her.

"Just drop them." She turned and walked away.

He trailed behind her. Something about the moment reminded him of the first night they'd spent together. Except, this time, he had on his pants. "Darling, I wasn't trying to intrude."

"You can leave now," she said as she took the longest strides her legs would allow across the yard away from him.

He needed to take control of the situation and her. "Darling, stop." People around them stared. "Is there someplace we can talk?"

She stopped and crossed her arms across her body. "About what?"

He wanted to drop the boxes, pick her up and fling her over his shoulder. If he could get her away from the gawking crowd maybe, he could get her to listen. "Darling, we should talk."

"I don't want to talk." She headed toward the backyard. "It's the weekend. I'm on my time, not yours."

"I thought I was invited." He kept following her. "But, I guess that part was a lie." He followed her into the modest home. They stood in the home's small dining room, which was tastefully decorated with a china cabinet filled with matching sets of plates and porcelain cups. The wood table in the center of the room only sat four. Big enough for Darling, her mother and father, plus one seat for a guest.

"What do you want?" she asked.

"I apologize if I shouldn't be here. But, I thought

Barbara called to tell you I was coming."

Darling leaned against the fridge behind her and crossed her arms underneath her small breasts. What she did in anger only tempted him. The gentle bounce of her breasts against her arms made him hunger for another opportunity to caress her nipples with his tongue and hear her moan for more of him.

"Well, she didn't. I don't even know how she knew where my parents lived."

He placed the boxes on the carpeted floor. "If you don't want us here, I'll grab mom and we'll leave." He left the kitchen feeling like one of the biggest idiots. How could he have fallen for Barbara's high school trick? Shit! He wanted to believe her. That's why. When he stepped into the backyard, he bumped into the woman that reminded him so much of Darling.

"Are you leaving?" she asked.

"Yes, ma'am." There was no reason for him to stay.

"You just got here. You can't leave. Your mom is reading to a group of the children." She grabbed his arm and led him back to the front yard. "We'll get you a plate and if you have time, you can relieve my husband on the grill."

As much as he'd love the chance to spend one more moment with Darling, he didn't want to be the laughing stock of the party. "I don't know if that's a good idea."

She squeezed his arm a little tighter. "It's a perfect idea." She dragged him over to the grill. "I'm Darling's mother, Shannon Crawford."

"I'm Jaxon."

"I know exactly who you are." She grinned as they came to a stop in front of the grill.

Mr. Crawford looked up from his duties as head chef. "So, you're my relief?"

Jaxon stared at the food and searched his memory for the last time he'd actually grilled anything. College. A mixer with one of the sororities. He'd gotten drunk and ended up in bed with someone he barely knew. Everything on the grill had burned. "I don't know about that sir, I'm not the best on the grill."

"Well, you better learn quick." He laughed. "This can be a mean crowd if you burn their smoked sausages."

Darling's angry steps crushed the grass beneath her feet as she neared the grill. "Mom, dad...what are you doing?"

"Honey, we needed a few more hands. Your dad needs a break." Her mom smiled at him. "Your friend Jaxon has agreed to help us out for a while." She allowed her eyes to sweep over the two of them. "Isn't that sweet?" she asked rhetorically.

"Mom, dad, this is my boss and that's his mother." She glanced over her shoulder at Jaxon's mom, and then shook her head. "They are just being nice. I'm sure they have something else to do with their day." Her eyes pleaded with Jaxon.

"Well, son, do you have something else to do?" her father asked.

For a moment, he watched his mother who had children of all ages mesmerized with whatever story she read as she hopped around like a kangaroo. "No, sir. I think we're fine."

"Great. Darling, you stay here and help him, while your mom and I take a break."

Darling's expression was a mixture of anger and sadness. "Dad—" she pleaded.

"Have fun, honey," her dad tossed the words into the air as he walked away with her mother.

As much as Darling wanted to see him, she didn't want to see him. Not here at her parents' home. She'd been running around barefoot and her hair looked a mess. Without checking herself out in a mirror, she felt sure that somewhere on her body, there was barbeque and orange soda compliments of Cedric. And in front of her stood the one man that both excited her and made her feel ashamed. "Jaxon, how could you believe Barbara, and show up here at my family's home?"

"I don't know what to say to you, but I—"

"But, what?" If she looked at him, she'd probably curse him out. She snatched the grilling fork from its resting place and used it to spear hot dogs and sausages before she tossed them into the empty aluminum pan she'd nearly crumpled. "But, what Jaxon?"

His head lowered, and he whispered against her ear. "I wanted it to be true."

The warmth of his breath against her skin confused her thoughts. What did he say? Why would he lie to her? "You wanted to spend your Sunday with me?" He had the model, and she was sure there were so many others that'd be more than willing to spend their Sunday with him.

He placed a hand on her left hip and took a step closer.

She took a step back and tried to take another, but he gave her hip a light squeeze, and she stopped. That touch reminded her of the night they'd spent dancing. She'd never be able to get this man out of her head.

He kept his mouth where it was. "I find myself thinking about you often and I enjoy spending time with you."

None of the events of the past weeks should've happened. No matter how much she'd enjoyed spending time with him, it made no sense. He and his mother didn't fit into her world. She watched his mother play with the children because she couldn't dare glance into his beautiful green eyes. Standing so near to him made her body buzz and her mind cloud. "Where's the blonde?" she asked. *Just curious.*

He took a step back and stared into her eyes. "There's no one."

It didn't matter how good those words made her feel, she knew she was right. "Jaxon, I thought we agreed."

He placed a hand on her chin and forced her to look at him. "No. I told you I would do what you wanted."

"Yes, but I thought you wanted it, too."

He dropped his hand to his side. "Damn it, Darling. You know it's not what I want."

"Jaxon, look at your mother. Look at me and my family." She didn't understand why this was so difficult for him. Couldn't he see what she saw? There was nothing she could offer him. They came from two different worlds. *Just like her and her ex.* Right now, she was interesting, but eventually he'd become bored with her, too. Or, think she and her family weren't good enough.

If they stopped it before it began, there would be no hard feelings.

"I'm looking at you, Darling." He put too much space between them and stuffed his fisted hands into the pockets of the shorts he wore. "What about you? Are you looking at me? My mother is having a great time, and I would be too, if…." He walked back to her side and slowly slid his hands down the length of her arms until he clasped her hand in his.

"You don't understand anything." Frustrated with him and herself, she pulled her hand free of his and damn near ran to the kitchen with the pan of food.

Before returning to his side, Darling stood near the back of the house and watched him. Even in shorts and a t-shirt, he could break any woman's heart. It would be so easy to let herself believe him and everything he said. But, she'd done that before, and look at what that got her. She was single and almost forty, while her ex began again with a woman ten years younger. There was no way she could go through not being good enough again.

The line of folks waiting at the grill smiled and talked as he dished out food. The women hovered a little too long and close. The woman who walked behind the grill, Lisa, was bold. Darling watched as the woman cooed at Jaxon, then picked up an apron and wrapped it around his waist, tying it in the back. What the…? Well, Darling may not know what she wanted, yet. But, she knew she didn't like Lisa touching him. Darling interrupted their conversation. "Hope I wasn't gone too long."

"No." Lisa smiled. "I was just helping him with the apron so he wouldn't spill anything on his shorts." The woman's hand wandered a little brushing Jaxon's thigh.

"Thank you," Jaxon said.

Lisa smiled as she walked away.

Darling stretched on her tiptoes to reach his ear. "You just let everybody touch you?"

For a minute, he stared without words. Then, a grin spread across his face. He placed his hand on her hip and dropped his head close to hers.

Her heart jumped in her chest. She didn't know what to do, he was about to kiss her right there in front of everyone. Her body reacted to the need for his kiss. Possessive. His kisses made her feel wanted. A dull throb ached between her legs for his touch as her breasts begged for the gentle firm suckle of his mouth. She should push him away. She could feel the smile curving his lips as he touched them against her cheek.

"Nobody has touched me since you left my bed."

The revelation frightened her.

"Darling, are you guys just going to stand back there, or give us something to eat?" asked someone in line.

Jaxon squeezed her hip as he severed their connection.

Darling shook her head in an attempt to shake off her madness, and focused on the line to find it longer than ever. But, the women in line weren't coming for what was on the grill. "Hmm. I'll go get some more supplies." When she returned, the freaking line had grown, more. *Horny chicks!* "Dad," she yelled as she passed him. "I think it's time you take your grill back."

With a huge grin, her father watched them from the picnic table he shared with her mother. But, he didn't make a move. "What? Why? I think your young man is doing okay."

"Dad," she pleaded.

"I think you two can handle it." He turned back to her mother placing a kiss on her cheek. "Oh, and bring out some of those desserts."

"Mom, help me. Please."

"Honey, I agree with your father."

If she didn't know better, she'd swear that her parents planned this with Barbara and his mother. Everyone seemed perfectly okay with the two millionaires grilling and reading children's books in the middle of the front yard with the big fat blow up swimming pool. Meanwhile, they probably had in-ground heated Infiniti pools at their homes.

The party died down with the sunset. Jaxon and his mom cleaned away the remaining pieces of scattered trash along-side Darling and her parents. It'd been a long time since he'd washed dishes without loading a dishwasher. But, Darling flipped the television to one of the music channels and everyone hummed along as they finished the duties her mother had assigned them.

"Thank you for helping." She handed him a plate of food wrapped in foil.

"It was my pleasure. Your parents are sweet."

"Sweet conspirators." She smiled.

"Why don't you two go and have fun. We can finish this," her mother said.

"That's a great idea, honey," Jaxon's mother agreed.

Have fun. A few quiet hours with Darling would be the perfect way to end the evening, there were so many things he'd love to do to her. He couldn't walk out on his mother.

"Jaxon don't worry about your mom. I'll take her home," Mr. Crawford added as if reading his mind.

They'd never made it to their game of tennis. His mother had spent the day entertaining twenty kids, and he'd cooked for all of them. "Sir, I can't let you do that. I'll take mom back to the hotel."

"We won't hear of it. You and your mom helped us out so much tonight," her mother said. "The least we can do is let you two have a few moments to yourselves."

"Mom, we don't have anything to talk about," Darling said.

"Well, go and find something," her mom urged, "Get out of here and let us finish this." Her mom fanned her hands at them pushing them out of the house.

Jaxon drove with no agenda. The plane that buzzed through the air overhead gave him an idea. Moments later, he pulled up to the lot he frequented as a child with his father. They'd sit for hours and watch the planes come and go. Maybe that's why the old man had a thing for stewardesses. The homes that used to line the perimeter were gone. Vaguely, he remembered something about the airport purchasing a bunch of homes and bulldozing them. But, the park they'd created fit his needs. Funny that all those years, he'd only been around the corner from the woman who left him breathless, he thought. "Your parents do that cook-out often?"

"Every year."

"You have a huge family."

"They're not really members of our family. They're church members and foster children." She opened the door and walked to the front of the car. "My parents have always volunteered or done something...anything anybody needed or asked of them."

He followed behind her tossing a jacket from the trunk of his rental car over the hood. Then, he lifted her and placed her on it. "Your family is loved by a lot of people"

"Everyone they meet." She smiled. Thoughtful silence preceded her words. "Yeah, for as long as I can remember, my parents have formally or informally taken in foster children."

"My mom does a lot of volunteering, too. " He sat on the hood beside her. "Recently, she was nominated and received an award for her work back home in Nashville."

"That's pretty awesome. Maybe that's why she gets along so well with my parents."

"Maybe."

"Why do you say that?"

Jaxon's mother threw herself into her charity work because she was a wonderful woman, but she'd also been lonely. Filling long empty days and longer lonely nights volunteering, he was sure, beat the hell out of crying over a cheating husband and a philandering son. "I think my mom did it to have something to do, instead of spending her days and nights alone."

"But, she still made a difference in people's lives, or they wouldn't have given her an award."

"I'm proud of her. I think what she's done is important." He thought about all the years his mother had spent fundraising for one cause or another. The time she'd spent working with her church's outreach programs. Her favorite project helped fund computer labs in inner-city schools, when she didn't raise the money she needed, she dipped deeper into her own pockets to reach her goal to have the project completed. "It's just that I know a lot of it is because of me."

"Don't be so sure our parents did it for different reasons," she whispered as she raised a hand in the air and squinted one eye shut. "After I left for school, I think my parents felt a little like empty nesters, and they had a ton of love to handout. Especially, because..."

"Because why?"

"I lost a sister, Charity, when she was three." She continued to squeeze something between her fingers. "You know as kids we'd lay on blankets in the front yard, while our parents watched over us, counting and squeezing stars." She laughed, somberly. "My sister thought she could help the planes fly by squishing the stars, then she'd put them back by unsquishing them." With tears in her eyes, she propped herself up on one elbow and rubbed at a faint scar on her leg. "Funny what kids believe, huh?"

"I'm sorry, Darling. I had no idea." He reached for the single tear dangling from her dark lashes, but it splashed to the hood of the car before he could brush it away. "No wonder your parents are so well loved. They put all the love they had for your sister into you and the community around them."

She nodded her head in agreement. "Your mom does the same."

She was right. But, the only problem was his mother hadn't lost him or his father to death. His father left for the woman that would say yes to anything, including sneaking around with a married man until she got what she wanted. He'd left out of shame for being that man's son. "I guess so."

She leaned back against the windshield. "My husband and I never had children." She paused. "At least, not together."

The fact that she hadn't had another man's children did make him happy. "Did the two of you try for kids?"

She crossed her legs at the ankles. "We did, but I guess it just wasn't meant to be." Darling patted the lower region of her stomach.

The innocent gesture instantly ignited a need deep inside of him. He remembered too well the feel of her soft warm skin as he'd rested his head there briefly before he'd moved further down her body. The lower he'd traveled, the more she'd moaned and begged for the touch of his tongue to her sex. But, he'd held out as long as he could. Torturing both himself and her.

Slowly, her one hand slid down her stomach to her right thigh. "I think that ship has sailed." She paused. "What about you?"

He dragged his eyes away from her hands and the

memories they touched before he embarrassed himself. "My mother wants me to be a father. But, I don't know what kind of father I'll be." The confession he'd shared with his mother he was now sharing with the woman he was sure he was beginning to fall in love with.

"Why? Because of your father?"

What could he tell a son about being a good husband or father? What could he tell a daughter about choosing a good man? He could show either pictures of himself and his father, and say don't be like or pick a man like us. "Because he wasn't there and I've spent more time doing anything and everything other than being a good man."

"Role model. That's a hard one. I don't know how good I'd be at that one either." She smiled. "Did you really come to my parents' house because you wanted to see me?"

"Yes."

"You could've called."

He placed his feet on the ground and stood, then he reached for her, pulling her down the length of the hood of the car. Her thighs rested on the outside of his. There were a lot of things he could and wanted to do with her in that position, but tonight he needed to look into her troubled brown eyes and talk. "Darling, if I would've called, you would have shot me down."

Her eyes fell to the ground, briefly. "Maybe."

"There's no maybe. I know we need to think about work, but I own the company. I don't know what's ahead, but if it came to it…you won't have to work."

She leaned back and lowered her torso, resting her weight onto her arms. "There's no way I'd ever stop working. I would never allow myself to be completely reliant on a man to take care of me and my children."

He rubbed his hands up and down the length of her bare legs. "So, you do still want children?" His heart beat a little faster as he waited for her response.

"If I can ever find what I'm looking for and besides

there's always adoption."

"What are you looking for?" He leaned a little closer spreading her legs a little wider.

Darling slid up the car away from him. The planes overhead stirred the air around them nearly drowning out her words. "I don't know."

The night breeze that wrapped around them mingled her perfume with his cologne and the earthiness of the nearby trees. The scent intoxicated him. "I don't think I knew what I was looking for, but now that I've met you...I want you to give me a chance." He leaned in a little more.

This time, she didn't move. "A chance for what? You're my boss, and my divorce isn't even final."

"Do we have to label it, or know much more than how we feel when we're around each other?"

She didn't respond quickly. "How do you feel?"

"I think about you a lot. When I think about the weeks and months ahead, I think about how you can be a part of them."

Her eyes fell to her stomach. "I don't know. I'm not sure."

Jaxon placed his hand underneath her chin and lifted her eyes to his. "Stop thinking so much." This time, her perfume reached out and grabbed him. He wanted to get closer. She might bite him, but he kissed her anyway. Instead of biting him, she teased him by only allowing him the quickest touch before she pulled away.

"I'm sorry." He moved to step back.

She reached for him and twisted her fingers into the folds of the t-shirt he wore. Tightening her grip, she pulled him to her. Lengthwise, they stretched out on the hood of his car. As the metal popped and pinged, they explored each other's bodies underneath the rumbles of the planes with only the trees around them to protect them from would-be onlookers.

The feel of her body excited him almost beyond his

control. As many nights as he'd dreamed of this moment again, he wasn't going to let it happen on the hood of his rental car. Pushing up from the car, he kept her body pressed hard against his own. Too close to his own climax, he broke her kiss. "Let's go back to my hotel."

Heavily hooded eyes began to clear as she slid her hands along her body assessing what he'd done. "Maybe, you should take me back to my parents' house before…"

She'd already changed her mind. "Before what?"

"Before we go too far."

"What's too far, Darling?" He continued to hold her close. "I want to be with you. And just now, I'm pretty sure you wanted to be with me too."

"I'm just not sure we should do this. Too much would change."

Whatever she wanted is what would be done, but damn he needed to hear her answer, so he wouldn't keep making a fool of himself. "If you want this to end right now, it will. I don't want to feel like I'm forcing myself on you."

She softly pushed him away, threw her legs over the side of the car and hopped down. "Let's go."

CHAPTER TWELVE

Darling wasn't sure how long they'd sat inside the car before Jaxon started the engine. But, when the engine roared something inside of her screamed. She lunged yanking the key from the ignition. "Why are you playing games with the poor divorcee?"

"What in the hell is that supposed to mean?" he asked with brows pinched and a thin-lipped expression.

The first night, she understood. They'd been drinking and dancing. But, he wasn't stopping. He didn't have to lie to her to get her into his bed. He'd already had her in his bed. "Why are you trying so hard to have sex with me?"

He held his hand out. "Give me my keys."

"Not until you explain why?" She didn't have time to be a temporary trophy for another man.

"Darling, if you think this is just about sex, we don't need to do this now or ever."

His words upset her more than she expected anything he said to her could. Damn it! Why did the hurt in his voice wound her, too? She wanted to feel the warm firmness of his chest against her body. She needed the comfort and safety of his arms as he'd offered the night she showed up at his hotel unannounced. "I'm sorry. I don't know…"

This stiffness of his back and the coldness of his expression softened. "Darling, I told you I want you. I'm not playing any sort of games with you. I know you're concerned because of the job."

"Concerned!" She threw the keys at him. "I pay my bills with the money you pay me. Sleeping with you would just make me a hooker." *Or, a fool.* Maybe both.

"Hooker?" He searched for the keys between his legs. "That's really what you think?"

"How would you describe it?"

He cranked up the car. "What do you want me to do? Fire you? Or, quit myself?"

She frowned as she let his statement sink in. What was he supposed to do? "That doesn't make sense."

"That's my point." He turned the car off. "I want you Darling, but I don't know what to do. Everything I try seems to be wrong." He rested his head against his headrest.

For the first time, Darling allowed her eyes to take their time. Not with a gaze filtered through the bottom of an empty vodka glass, or from across a conference table, or through a crowd of women lined up at a grill waiting for seconds, but unhindered by anything except her heart— she took in all of him. From the black curls of his hair, some kissed with hints of grey, to his thick brows, fuller nose, well-kept mustached mouth—he was gorgeous. His eyes were closed, but when they opened and he turned his gaze toward her, she wanted to twist her fingers through the curls of his hair, grab hold and pull him close. "You don't understand," she said.

"Then how about you explain it to me."

The sincerity of his green gaze fired through her. "It's too late to drag out my past." Darling closed her eyes and inhaled deeply. It'd been months, but still nausea rolled over her at the thought of Steve loving another. Why? She didn't love him. She didn't hate him. She just didn't. Not anymore. "I'm tired of it all."

"Darling, what...tell me? What do you need from me?"

"I've been down this road before."

"What road?"

The warmth of his hand to her cheek both calmed and excited her body.

"Open your eyes. Talk to me."

She wanted to cry. Not for Steve. But, for herself. It'd been too long since she'd allowed herself the tenderness of a man. The kindness. The warmth. As the memories of her life with Steve flooded her mind, she began to hope a little that what Jaxon offered might be real. "It feels like ages ago—when he came into my life." She moved his hand from her face to her lap and held it between her own. His nearness grounded her in reality and provided her contact that she desperately needed. "He was what I thought I wanted in a man and I fought hard for him..."

"You fought for him?"

She grinned at the memories of her beauty routine: waxing, plucking, skin treatments, hair treatments and whatever she thought needed to be done to keep Steve's attention. "Not literally...more preventative. I guess."

"Why did you have to fight so hard?"

"Because Steve thought he needed a woman on his arm that every other man envied. Someone who looked like they could've walked off the pages of a magazine."

"So, you tried to be that woman?"

"Every moment of every day." She traced a finger over the lines on the palm of his hand. "When we were first married, I'd wake up before him just to be sure I showered, brushed my teeth and did my hair before breakfast."

"Darling—"

She nodded her head in agreement with his thoughts.

"No, I know it's pretty stupid. It was probably about four years into our marriage before I felt comfortable enough to sleep in late." *Maybe I never should've gotten that comfortable, or maybe I never should've been with a man that made me so uncomfortable that I couldn't be myself.*

"Baby, none of what you're telling me is stupid." He caressed her cheek with the hand she wasn't squeezing between her own. "You loved him."

Baby. The word warmed her from the inside and encouraged her. Holding his hand wasn't enough. She wanted so much more of him. "But, my point is…he used to chase me and act a lot like you."

"Like me." The reassuring warmth of his touch left her grip. "Don't compare me to him. You haven't given me a chance and you're telling me, it's because I'm telling you that I want you."

"It's because you act like there's something special or different—about me." She stared into his eyes. "There isn't."

"You are special. When I walked up to you in that bar, it was because you were the only woman in the room not scoping out the crowd. You weren't doing anything but enjoying the music, and I loved watching you move to it. I won't lie and say I didn't think you were sexy." His hand rubbed the length of her thigh. "I'll have that red dress etched in my mind for a long, long time. But, when you walked out on me the next morning, I felt like an idiot."

"That wasn't about you." She wanted to leave before he told her some stupid lie to get her to leave. He'd told her he wasn't married, but that didn't mean he didn't have someone somewhere. That night had been such a rush of emotions. The carriage ride. The dance. The drinks. He'd given her more romance than she'd received from her ex the last years of their marriage. It was a fantasy. One she'd thought could never be anything more than what it had been.

"I've had a lot of one-night stands. I'm usually the one

leaving…not the woman." He remained just out of her reach. "You didn't tell me anything. Just dressed and left."

"Oh, I hurt your ego?" A man like him couldn't be used and forgotten by a woman like her.

"Of course, what man wouldn't be? You make love to a beautiful woman and the next morning, she practically runs from your bed. But, when I found you again…I thought maybe we could—"

"What?" she asked. "Pick up where we left off?" How would that work? Walk into the boss' office for lunch and have a little noon-time quickie.

"Dumb. Yes, I know, but I couldn't stop thinking about you…no matter who I was with or what I was doing."

"Not just sex or the excitement of screwing your employee."

"Screwing my employee. Damn." Anger and disappointment crossed his face.

Maybe, she was pushing him further away, but she needed to know. "But, is it true?"

"No. I've never slept with anyone who works for me. To be fair, when we were together, you didn't work for me."

Even as she spoke her next words, relief spread through her body. "None of this matters because I do now." She let her head rest against the glass of the passenger side window. "It would all be too complicated." She watched her breath fog the window and fade with each word she spoke.

"It matters if you want to be with me." He paused. The touch of his hand against her thigh pulled her eyes to his. "Do you want to be with me?"

Something inside of her kept tugging her heart toward him. No matter how much she wrestled with it, she lost more and more ground. "I don't know."

He looked at her with disbelief. "Don't know or scared?"

Each word he spoke cleared her thoughts and set her on a path she didn't think she could control. "Jaxon, I've been hurt so badly. How many times can hearts heal, completely?"

Jaxon stared into the brown eyes of the woman who was quickly beginning to take over his every thought and action. The frown lines that creased the beautiful dark skin of her forehead betrayed the words she spoke. "Darling, I'm uncertain, too, but I need you to be honest with me. I don't know what to do if you don't tell me something other than lies."

"Lies?" The beautiful dark lashes trimming her eyes fluttered as she blinked away tears.

Jaxon never wanted anything more in his life than he did in that moment. He wanted to hold her. To kiss away the tears in her eyes. To always be the person she'd turn to when she wanted to be held. He needed to be that person. "Yes. I think you know what you want, but you're scared to admit it."

"You think you know me well enough to call me a liar."

He leaned closer and she jumped in her seat. "Yes." He smiled. "Where you afraid I was going to kiss you?"

"No." She frowned.

"Good." He leaned in again, but this time, he did kiss her.

The stiffness of her body melted away, the longer he kissed her. She pushed her body into his asking for more and more.

The more she wanted, the more he gave. Grass, earth, hickory, smoke and something else…vanilla flooded his senses. The softness of her breasts against his chest made his body burn. The memories of their night together burst into his mind.

The small fingers of her hand stroked his thigh

massaging its way closer to the sensitive tip of his penis that longed to be caressed by her tongue. At the gentle touch of her fingers to the fabric restraining the delicate tip of his organ, he grabbed her hand and held on tight. He broke their kiss and whispered against her ear. "Let's go to my hotel." His voice came out husky and promising.

Darling didn't respond to him, but instead, took his mouth as she slid her fingers free from his grasp. Shoving away the cotton of his shorts, she pushed her hand along his thigh until she found what she wanted. Gently, she dragged her nails over the tip of his penis.

The sensation rocketed through his body. He needed her touch too much to have her tease. "Darling, I—" The sliding sound of his zipper stopped his words. His cock twitched at the touch of her small hand. He grew harder as her fingers wrapped around the thickness of his rod and possessively stroked him into a hazy fog. He stopped kissing her and stared into her eyes. "You sure you want to do this here?" He didn't have enough restraint left to continue to control himself or the situation.

Her cloudy eyes tried to focus. "I want you."

Jaxon couldn't pull his eyes away from her full moist lips pouty from kissing. "Get in the back." The words were almost a command.

She knew it. A grin crossed her face as she looked into his eyes.

Damn, her mouth kept teasing him. Before the night ended, he'd be sure he showed her how much he loved it.

She scrambled from her seat to the back, but he had to exit the car after tucking himself back into this pants.

In the backseat, she'd stripped from the shorts that had teased him all night and her t-shirt.

Jaxon stood where he was and watched as Darling took two fingers of one hand and slowly slid them along her clit before pushing them into the warmth of her body. She smiled at him as she arched her back and moaned. Her slit glistened as she pulled the fingers out exposing the beautiful shaved folds of her body to him. Her chocolate skin had the subtlest touch of pink.

His hand fell to his cock. He massaged it through the cloth of his shorts as his eyes drank in the woman waiting for him.

Intoxicated by the sight of her body, he crawled into the back seat. As he kissed her, he let his hand explore the soft wetness of her body. With each push of his fingers, she breathed a warm breath into her kiss. When her legs tightened against his hand while she began to grind against his fingers, he broke away and unzipped his pants. Propped against the seat, he pulled her on top of him. The need growing inside of him set his pace. He slipped the soft sensitive tip of his rod into her. The feel of her wet warm body as it stretched to sheath him excited him and he pushed harder, deeper.

His memories of her didn't compare to this reality, and he couldn't control the urgency within him to take her. He drove into her...hard. With her mouth open and the power of his thrust, Darling threw her head back. There was so much he could do to that mouth. As he imagined her full lips wrapped around his full erection, he thrust harder and harder. The temptation of her mouth forced him to reach a hand behind her head, and pull her mouth to his. Wet and warm, her tongue battled with his until she pushed him into the car seat, and trailed kisses down his neck to his torso.

She focused on his mouth again, but he leaned her back against the seat behind her, and took one of her nipples into his mouth. The sound she made when his tongue brushed across her distended nipple excited him, quickening his rhythm and thickening him inside of her. With her nipple in his mouth, he slowly relaxed against the seat behind him, and she followed pressing the full weight of her small full breast into his mouth for his pleasure and hers.

He couldn't hold on much longer. The slow forceful

circular motion of her hips pushed him over the edge.

She stared into his eyes as she pushed her hands against his shoulders and rocked against his body.

He gripped her butt and pulled her against him, hard and tight.

Arching her back, she teased him with the sight of her breasts as she reached her hands over her head and used the seat behind her to assist her as she gyrated her body against his.

"Darling…"

Harder and harder, she rode him.

He took one of her breasts into his mouth again and her whole body trembled in his arms. The feel of her uncontrollable spasms around his rod excited him and he thrust deeper inside of her, releasing his own orgasm.

She collapsed against his chest breathing heavily and he wrapped his arms around her. He held on because even though she had nowhere to run, he never wanted to let her go.

CHAPTER THIRTEEN

Jaxon wrapped his arm around Darling's warm naked body as she lay sleeping beside him. He'd known that if he ever gave in to what he felt...it would cripple him. And damn, if it hadn't. Every morning he woke since the night of the cookout, he thought he would wake alone, but not yet. The fear of her walking away had the power to crush his heart. She'd asked him how many times a heart could heal. He didn't know and didn't want to find out, if it meant he would ever lose her.

He kissed her softly on the cheek. "Breakfast?"

She wrapped herself tighter in his arms. "Please," she mumbled. "I'm really hungry," she said as she kissed the wrist of the arm closest to her mouth.

"Waffles and eggs?" he asked.

"That sounds good, but can you add steak...yeah, steak and eggs, and grits with sugar and butter." She turned to look into his eyes and gave him a good morning kiss.

He loved the way her dark hair spread across her face in the mornings. He always knew which side she'd slept because that side would be slightly puffier than the rest of her hair, if she didn't hide it away in a scarf. He definitely preferred it just as it was, because when he held her at night he could bury his face in her hair and be reminded by the wonderful hint of vanilla that she wasn't a fantasy. There were even a few nights when she hadn't been there that he'd asked housekeeping to leave everything alone, so that vanilla scent of hers wasn't erased from his pillow cases or sheets.

He rolled over in bed, grabbed the phone and placed their orders. If he'd ever done anything right in his life, it'd been to book a room at The Peabody, which was legendary for many reasons. One of them was its brunch.

A half hour later and amazed at how much food such a small woman could put away, Jaxon watched Darling finish her plate before she stole a forkful or two of his with a smile.

She shrugged her shoulders. "I don't know I guess I was really starved." She smiled. "It's your fault. You wouldn't let me sleep last night."

He kissed her on the cheek as he headed toward the bathroom to shower. "I don't plan on letting you sleep tonight, either." That was a promise. Now that he could have her, he wanted her all the time. *Why wait?* "I'm going to hop in the shower before I pick my mom up for tennis." He looked over his shoulder. "Join me."

The smile that broke across her face as she stood shot straight through him. Could he ever get used to not seeing that smile when he woke? He didn't want to think about it; instead, he focused on the beautiful wild-haired woman walking toward him wearing nothing but a smile. This was going to be a really good morning.

Darling stepped under the warm spray of the shower. The power of the water beat down on her shoulders relaxing her even more than the tasty eggs and steak. Jaxon stood at the other end of the shower waiting for her; his naked body enticing her. Lately, it didn't seem like she needed much, but Jaxon's desire always welcomed her advances no matter where or when.

His touch to her sensitive breasts sent a shiver through her body that she couldn't remember feeling before, but she wanted to feel it again and again. No matter how many times she told the man not to get her hair wet, he did; but, this time she didn't care. He lifted her and leaned her against the shower wall. Hot water from the shower matted her hair to her face and shoulders, but he brushed it away as he kissed her cheek and neck. The touch of his lips against her skin heated her more than the steam from the shower.

He held her tight as she bucked against him and the warm shower tiles. Jaxon filled her so completely, but still she craved so much more. He placed her on the tiles of the shower floor, and lowered himself down on top of her.

The wait for his touch made her reach out for him and pull him into her kiss.

His moans as he deepened his thrusts inside her increased her need and to satisfy it, she wrapped one leg around him and took every powerful thrust. The ache in her breasts assisted by the hard warm spray of the shower tightened and firmed her nipples, begging for the warmth of his mouth and the tenderness of his tongue. A subtle push of his head gave him the signal he needed.

She ran her fingers through the wet strands of his hair, holding him tight to her as she kissed him. The weight of his body on top of hers comforted her. She never wanted to lose it, or him. Her leg tightened around him locking their bodies together as her orgasm burst through her, followed by the pulsating thrusts that told her he'd climaxed. Her need for Jaxon was more than sex. Her heart was losing the battle against him. She wrapped both legs around him, and let the water beat down on them as she listened to the rhythm of his breathing.

How could she ever let him go?

Dressed in her tennis whites, Jaxon's mother lobbed tennis balls at him with the strength of a woman half her age. A couple of matches a week had become part of their normal routine since he'd been staying in Memphis. Especially with Rodney back, he didn't need to be in the office as much. His relationship with Darling was easier to conceal with one of them out of the building.

"Mom, let's take a break," he yelled across the court.

She waved her racquet as she responded, "Okay."

He grabbed his towel and they walked to a canopied table to order drinks. But, before he could have the first taste of the cold glass of tea in front of him, his mother asked, "Son, how much longer are you going to drag your feet with Darling, and fabricate reasons to be in Memphis?"

"Am I that obvious?"

"To anybody watching."

"She's been through a lot." He finally had a drink of his sweet tea. "If I push too hard, she'll run."

"What about you?" His mother stared at him with a look of hope.

He grew more confident every day in what he wanted. "I want to be with her, but...her ex-husband...Their divorce finalizes soon. He and his new wife are keeping the house he built with Darling to raise their new family."

His mother squinted against the sun as she watched another match on the court in front of them. "Poor girl," his mother said with a shake of her head.

"They tried for kids for years, but nothing worked. Now, he has a new family and raising it in the house she dreamed their family would live."

"That's a lot for you to fight against." His mom rattled

the ice in her glass of tea emphasizing her words.

He knew it would be difficult, but wasn't that the mark of anything worth having? "I want...her."

His mother's glass of tea slipped from her hands against the table and cracked on the ground.

He pushed up from his seat, but his mom waved him off. "Mom, are you okay."

One of the waiters hustled over to the spill and for some reason, apologized to them for his mother's spill as he cleaned it up.

"I'm so sorry," his mother said. "My son surprised me," she said to the waiter with a smile. "Son, I've been waiting so long to hear you say those words about someone, but do you want her because you love her?"

"I've loved her for a long time. I didn't want to admit it to myself, but every moment I spend away from her gets harder and harder." He sipped from his tea. "I don't want to scare her away," he paused. "But, I've never felt this way about anyone."

His mother's hand covered his. "Son, as long as you're honest with her, you won't scare her." Her eyes fell to the ground before locking onto his. "Be honest. Be patient."

CHAPTER FOURTEEN

Darling cursed the chef at the dive near the office as she rushed to the bathroom. The green tea she'd wolfed back did nothing to calm her stomach. Straddling the toilet, she promised to never eat there again. Her stomach cramped in agreement at the memory. "Ugh," she moaned as she leaned her head against the stall door. She was thankful Jaxon had a great cleaning staff; otherwise, it could be a whole lot worse. The smell of pine actually helped to soothe her stomach.

"Who's that? Are you okay?" The question was filled with curiosity, more than concern.

Go away! "I'm fine."

"Darling?"

She stood and flushed the toilet. Wiping her mouth with a huge wad of tissue because the freaking roll wouldn't stop, she tossed it into a nearby garbage can as she focused and eased to the sink on wobbly legs. "Barbara, I'm fine. Thanks."

Darling didn't have to look at Barbara to know that her

eyes scanned her whole body. She could feel it.

"What's wrong with you? Are you contagious?" Barbara's eyes drilled her as she took a few steps backwards.

"No, I'm not contagious. I ate something bad at lunch." She tried to force a smile.

"You sure. You don't look well at all." Barbara frowned.

"Thanks, but I'm okay." She splashed some water on her face. "But, I think I might go home early. Can you handle the office?"

Barbara didn't say anything. She kept staring like she knew something that Darling didn't. "You sure you're not pregnant?"

"What?" *Pregnant!* She hadn't thought of that. There was no way she could be. She and Steve had tried for children for years. She'd wanted to try IVF, but Steve said it wasn't worth it to spend so much money. According to him, they were too old and should focus on everything else, instead of wasting money on children.

People would think we are our own children's grandparents. Guess that was not the case with his new wife.

"No. I'm not pregnant."

I'll buy a pregnancy test on the way to my parents' house.

Hours later, surrounded by plastic wrappers from three pregnancy tests tossed without care around her tiny room and shreds of the inconspicuous little brown bag that shielded them from her parents' eyes as she'd carried them into the house, Darling cried. Curled up in the middle of the bed she'd slept in as a kid, she wept until her body shook the mattress beneath her. How had they been so careless? How could she be pregnant at her age? Her divorce wasn't final. She lived with her parents and she was sleeping with her boss.

Great freaking role model!

How would she tell her parents? Jaxon?

Just thinking about it, it seemed impossible, but Jaxon

might think she planned it. That she tried to *trap* him. He would hate her.

###

A week had passed, and Jaxon still hadn't seen Darling. The phone calls and texts weren't enough. She'd told Rodney she hadn't been feeling well and would need some time off. But, Jaxon didn't think that meant time off from him, too. No matter the problem, they were one now, or he thought they were. He rubbed at the ache in his chest. What was he supposed to do if she was walking out of his life?

He knocked at the door and waited.

Her father stood without his normal jovial smile. "Hi, son."

"Hi, Mr. Crawford." He glanced through the doorway, searching. "Is Darling here?"

The grey haired man folded his arms across his rounded belly. "No, son, I'm sorry. She went to visit her girlfriend, Annette, in Charlotte."

What the hell! Why would she leave the city without telling him?

Mr. Crawford stood waiting and watching while he kicked around different scenarios in his head.

None of the scenarios made any sense. "Charlotte?"

The man's arms slowly fell to his side. "I'm picking her up from the airport tomorrow."

"Airport." Now, even he thought he was beginning to sound stupid.

"Son, you don't have a lot to say do you?" Mr. Crawford stepped back. "Come on in."

He didn't know what to say or do. She'd left town without a word. Images of the past month flew through his mind. Dinners. Dancing. Waking up beside her. Nothing was out of place. There could be no mistaking the meaning behind her kiss or touch. What had he missed that would make her leave Memphis, him, without saying anything. "Sir, I don't want to disturb you and Mrs. Crawford." Maybe she realized she didn't love him? Maybe this was her way of sparing him the face-to-face bullshit of cutting her ties.

He turned to leave.

"Mrs. Crawford isn't here," the older gentleman said as Jaxon turned. "She's at church. But, you can keep me company. It's been a little lonely around here without my Darling." Jaxon stepped inside, and Mr. Crawford closed the door. "But, I guess it won't be quiet much longer."

"I guess not…not when she returns." When she returns to tell him to leave her the hell alone and to not show up at her parents' home. He knew this shit would happen. This is why he didn't want to take the fucking chance. He followed behind Mr. Crawford cursing himself for being stupid enough to think it all might work out in his favor.

The old man wound his way through a living room too tight for the furniture pushed against every wall to a smaller room off to the left. The room wasn't much bigger, but had considerably less furniture. It had only a couple of reclining chairs, a stereo system straight out of the nineties, and a TV from the latest Sears catalogue.

Mr. Crawford stopped in front of the TV and scanned the room. He located the remote and picked it up from its resting place on one of the chairs. "I'll be glad when she's back. I know you must be anxious." He offered Jaxon a guarded smile.

"Anxious?" Angry. Yes. But, anxious. Why would he be anxious?

Mr. Crawford stared with an odd expression between disbelief and question. He stopped switching channels. "Do you like karate?"

"Mr. Crawford I didn't know she'd left town?" He waited for a response. When none came, he continued. "Do you know why she left?"

Mr. Crawford glanced up at him as he lowered himself into one of the recliners. If he didn't know the older man was in his sixties, he would've given him about fifty-two or three. Not one wrinkle creased his dark skin.

Normally, her father greets him with a smile. Today, that didn't happen. But, for a split second, it was there and then it was gone. "Son, it looks like you and my daughter have a lot to talk about when she returns."

"Yes, sir, we do." He sat in the available seat beside Mr. Crawford and stared at the images dancing across the television screen. He'd seen the movie before. The son avenged the death of his father by chasing the ninjas who'd assassinated him. Somewhere in the middle of all of it, the son met and fell in love with the daughter of the man who'd killed his father. He didn't remember how it ended, but he'd be willing to bet not well for the son. How could it? He had to kill the father of the woman he loved, or he wouldn't avenge his father's murder.

No way to win. Not even in a movie.

"Son, how do you feel about my daughter?" Darling's father muted the television and waited.

There was only one answer to the question, but at that moment, he felt like a sixteen year-old craving the approval of his girlfriend's father. And he was confident that Mr. Crawford knew exactly why Darling had left town. He needed to know what the other man knew. "Sir?"

Mr. Crawford focused his attention on Jaxon. "How do you feel about my daughter?" He smiled. "And call me Roy."

Heat spread across Jaxon's chest as he loosened his tie. "I—sir, Roy, I'm in love with her, but—"

This time, Mr. Crawford did smile and clicked the volume up on the TV. "But, what?"

"I don't know if she's ready to hear me say that I love her." He pressed again. "Sir, do you know why she left town?"

Roy nodded his head as if considering his response.

The colors of the television screen reflected against a small shiny bald spot on top of the man's head. "Maybe, but she needs to know that a man can love her no matter what. Steve wasn't a bad man, but he didn't really love my daughter. He loved the way she looked, her education...But, not really her."

"Sir, I love her. I want to be with her. My father left my mother and me when I was young. I never thought I'd find anyone I wanted to be with for life." Admitting he and his father were pricks to the father of the woman he loved was crazy. "But, from the moment I met Darling, she challenged me. She didn't make it easy, but, sir, I love her."

"How do you know you love her?" he asked.

"I've never wanted to see someone smile as much as I want to see her smile. And I'll do whatever it takes to make sure she's happy." He stared into the old man's eyes. "I want a family with her. I know that's been problematic in the past, but even if it means adoption, we can do it."

"Yes, I think you can." He smiled as he leaned back into the chair. "Enjoy the movie, son."

Jaxon had looped the Memphis International Airport a few times before he finally decided to park and sit on a bench to wait for Darling. After his night with Roy, they'd voted against Mrs. Crawford, Shannon, and decided he should pick Darling up from the airport. Neither would tell him why one agreed with him and why one objected. Roy ended the debate by stressing that Darling need to begin '...facing her problems.'" He wasn't sure what that meant, but Shannon agreed and the debate was over.

Darling walked right past him with her cell phone in hand.

"Darling."

She swung around.

He didn't know if it was because he hadn't seen her in a

week or because she was simply the most beautiful woman he'd ever known, but damn—she glowed. The dress she wore was made from stretchy cotton that hugged her breasts, which looked fuller, and rested against her round hips before ending mid-thigh. If he didn't think she'd scream for the police, he'd pull her into his arms and kiss her until onlookers made him stop. He'd hold her tight in his embrace until she grew tired of being in his arms, which he hoped would never happen.

"What are you doing here?" She shoved her phone into her purse.

"Your father asked me to pick you up." He scanned her. "I thought you were sick. Why did you leave without telling me?" He closed the distance between them. Her scent had changed. No longer fresh vanilla. Now, there was something else. Something a little sweeter with vanilla. Honey.

She stepped away and jerked her eyes from his. "Where are you parked?"

He grabbed her suitcase and led the way. The sound of the rollers of the luggage against the asphalt was the only thing that filled the air around them, except for the unspoken anger trapped inside him. He'd put as much on the line as she had. He deserved to know what the hell was going on.

At the car, he said, "We need to talk."

She continued to avoid his stare or the slightest contact. "Yes, we do, but I'm tired. Can we do it tomorrow?"

"No." He set the suitcase in the back and rounded the car to hold the door for her. "No, it's been a week. You owe me an explanation."

Inside of Jaxon's hotel room, Darling rehearsed her lines. How could she tell a man she'd only known for a handful of months that she was pregnant? There was no easy way to start this conversation. She watched as he poured a glass of her favorite wine and walked toward her.

She shook her head no. "No, thanks."

He placed both glasses of wine on the table in front of the couch where she waited, and sat beside her. "What's going on?"

A week to prepare yourself to tell a man life-changing information that you barely believed wasn't enough time. She could and would raise their child by herself, but she refused to be one of those women who popped up ten years later on Father's Day and yelled, "Surprise!"

"I'm pregnant." Might as well throw it out there and see if he kicks her out, or asks for a paternity test. Hell, even she didn't think she could get pregnant, normally.

"Pregnant?" He grabbed his glass of wine and drank, then replied, "You sure?"

"Of course. That's why I've been missing in action? I've been trying to decide what I want to do. I didn't know how to tell you."

He sat drinking from the glass he held until every ounce of the delicious red wine had vanished. "And what do you want to do?"

"I want this baby." She threw up her hands as she stood to stop him from interrupting. She paced as she spoke, "Listen. I don't expect anything from you. Nothing." She stared at her glass of wine. She'd love a sip to calm her nerves. "I can do this by myself with the help of my family. But, I wanted you to know."

"You thought I should know that you're pregnant with my baby, but you want to raise it without me?"

The gravity of his words slammed into her stomach. She hadn't meant to take away anything from him. She just didn't want to make him feel obligated to her or the baby. "I don't want to raise the baby without you. But, I—"

He sat his glass on the table. "You do a lot of thinking for me." The words were tinged with anger.

She found it easier to focus on anything in the room, but him. The pressure of his stare made her want to cry and apologize until he forgave her. "I'm not thinking—"

"Yes, for me. Stop thinking for me and include me," his voice lowered.

She would do anything to erase the hurt from his voice. "I thought you—"

"That's my point…you thought." He pushed the glass further away, then stood and took her hands into his. "I'm in love with you. I've been losing my mind over the last week. I didn't know what was wrong and those messages you left didn't tell me anything." His fingers threaded through the locs of her hair before sliding down her arms back to their original position. "I thought I'd lost you."

"I didn't want you to be with me because I was pregnant—or, think I was trying to—to trap you."

"Darling, you've done nothing, but run from me since we met. I've been chasing you around for months. I know you couldn't get pregnant with your ex. Why would I think you planned this?" He paused. "I'm equally responsible. We didn't use condoms. I wanted to feel you," he said in a voice a little huskier than before. His hands tightened around hers. "I wouldn't change any of that."

"I'm such a mess." She pulled her hands from his and covered her face. Her embarrassment at her own stupidity made her want to disappear. She moved to put some space between them, but he pulled her back to him. Briefly, he held her against his chest. The firmness of him against her made her feel safe. Loved. She could hear the beat of his heart and wondered if their child's heartbeat would have that same soft rhythm. Then, he took a step back. She wanted to wrap her arms around his waist and hold on. She didn't want him to let her go.

"You don't get to keep running." He nodded at her belly. "Not from me. Not now."

"I didn't mean to run, but I didn't want to make you feel like you owed me anything."

"I don't do anything I don't want to do."

Everything he said, she'd hoped to hear, but hearing it didn't seem real. A man who wanted her...wanted the child that grew inside her. Her hand went to her stomach. "I've wanted a baby for so many years, but it never happened. Then, you come into my life and in a matter of months, I'm pregnant." Tears fell. "With your baby." Her hand rubbed in small circles on her belly. "I want our baby."

He smiled. "I wanted us," he paused. "And eventually, I'd hoped we'd start a family together, but I was afraid of what kind of father I'd be."

Her hand went to his cheek. She hadn't thought he'd have doubts about how good of a father he'd make. She just didn't think he'd want to be a father at all. Especially, not with her. A woman who had nothing. A woman who was the same age as him. "I thought—I thought you would leave me."

"I know what you thought and why." He kissed her forehead. "But, I don't plan on going anywhere. *Ever.*" A slow grin slid across his face as he lowered himself to the couch pulling her with him. He leaned into her pressing the weight of his body into hers.

His kisses stole away her breath. The strength of him, his kiss, was just as she remembered. She'd missed him so. She broke his kiss. "We haven't finished talking."

Gentle kisses covered her face until he moved down her throat to the top of her breasts. "You've been gone for a week. We need to do a lot of things." He continued to cover her with kisses, pulling at the soft cotton of her dress where it rested against her thighs. "Do you think I can get you pregnant again?" He laughed.

The feel of his warm breath and the gentle tease of his teeth as he toyed with her aching nipples ignited a desire deep within her that was only for him. "Maybe." She laughed. "Let's try." She fisted a hand in his hair, and held on.

CHAPTER FIFTEEN

Darling blinked at the bright light of the sun twinkling off the crystals sewn into the bodice of the dress resting in the trunk of her car. Surrounded by in-line skates and helmets, tennis racquets and balls, the dress fit perfectly with the other relics of her marriage. One last time, she ran her fingers along the length of the beautiful white fabric and marveled at its soft silky resilience. Unlike her marriage, the dress had managed to withstand being tossed around in storage and in her trunk. For a few dollars, the dry cleaners cleaned and pressed it and now, the dress would hopefully, bring someone else the joy she felt on her wedding day without the pain.

She delicately slid her arms underneath the wedding dress and hoisted it from the trunk of her car. She closed the trunk and strolled through the automatic doors of her favorite consignment shop. It was time she once and for all put the past behind her.

With the receipt for the wedding dress in her pocket for inspiration, Darling floated through the hallways of Slater Enterprises with her divorce papers signed and sealed. Time to have them delivered! Nothing had ever looked more beautiful than the mailroom and Darren, her new favorite person.

She sucked in a long deep breath as his fingers wrapped around the thin package and slowly pulled it from her hand. The weight of months of anxiety resting on her shoulders disappeared with the package's release. A knot formed in the pit of her belly as she turned to leave the room, not because of what she'd done, but because of what was next. The day had only just begun; she mentally prepared for her meeting.

Rodney and Barbara sat opened mouth as they listened to the options on the table.

"Texas. I don't know anyone in Texas. My children, my wife. Their home is here. We'd have to find a new home. New schools." Rodney thrust a hand through what hair he had as he spoke. "What am I supposed to do?"

"Your wife. Who cares about you and your damn wife?" Barbara's face crunched into a twist of anger and disbelief. "What about me? What happens to me?" She threw the words at everyone in the room with harsh anger.

Darling jumped into the conversation to ease Barbara's mind and to stop her from talking, "Barbara, I've worked with you and I think you could step into my role after I leave for Nashville." She watched as Jaxon leaned forward in his chair with his eyes locked on Barbara. Until then, he'd been focused on Rodney. Darling never had anything against Barbara. She actually thought Barbara was skilled at what she did when she wasn't on her back. The woman needed to keep it in her pants and stop throwing everything she had at Jaxon. Maybe she should've let Barbara think about it a little longer.

"What?" Barbara's snarl disappeared. Frown lines creased her forehead. "Is this a joke of some kind?"

"No," Jaxon said as he leaned back and relaxed a little. "Darling has provided me with enough to convince me that with her oversight, and without Rodney, you should be able to manage this office for Slater Enterprises."

"But, why—" Barbara began. Wide-eyed, she pivoted her attention between the two of them, and threw a few is-this-really-happening glances at Rodney.

"I think your experience with national programs and forecasting needs to grow, but I believe we can do it together." Darling chose her words, but everyone knew the blame rested with Rodney. "I think unnecessary distractions sidelined you and devalued your experience and knowledge."

"I—I don't know what to say." Barbara swiveled her chair toward Darling. She glanced down at the ring on Darling's finger. "I thought I knew exactly what type of woman you were. But, I was wrong. I'm sorry." Her head dipped a little. "I misjudged you." She blinked away tears. "Mr. Slater, I don't know how to apologize to you. To both of you."

"You don't owe me an apology," he said. "But, I need to know that you can dedicate yourself to this role." He glanced at Darling. "She believes you can do it. Prove her right."

Barbara nodded in agreement. "I will."

Darling extended her hand. "So, we're a team." She smiled.

"Team." Barbara accepted her gesture with a smile of her own.

Slicing his eyes across the room, Rodney said, "Barbara gets my job. Darling goes to Nashville and me—I'm shipped off to Texas." He rocketed from his chair and stormed from the office followed, quietly by Barbara.

Finally alone, Darling and Jaxon stood in the middle of the office. Rodney could stir up trouble in Texas. Maybe, he'd conjure up something, call a lawyer, and try to slap Jaxon with a lawsuit. Even if there were no grounds for it, the act of going to court or even settling out of court may soil the name of Slater Enterprises. "Do you think Rodney will be a problem?" she asked.

Jaxon laced his fingers with hers and lead her to the chair behind his desk. "No, I'll make sure human resources talks with him. Lay out his options, so that he has a complete understanding." He sat and pulled her down to his lap.

"Are you sure?" Because she wasn't. And there was no way she'd allow herself to be a pawn that Rodney could use against Jaxon. She wrapped her arms around his neck and leaned in until her forehead touched his. She inhaled long and slow. She loved the scent of him, a mixture of mandarin and persimmon "Are you really sure?"

"Don't worry about it. We've done everything as HR told us." He stroked a hand up and down her arm. "The rest is up to Rodney."

Darling closed her eyes and replayed the months since Steve uttered the words that'd changed her life. She'd left North Carolina, moved in with her parents and thought life was over. Too much of that time had been spent waiting. Waiting on Steve to chase after her and beg her to come back home. But, it'd never happened and she'd had to figure out how to drag herself out of bed and put one foot in front of the other one until she could stand. Even if it was on weaker legs.

Interviews had sucked because how can you convince someone to hire you when you're not sure of what you have to give. Not because she wouldn't work hard or be able to do the job, but because she left her desire for life in North Carolina with her ex and his new wife. Or, at least she thought she had.

She stared into the eyes of the man she loved. There was still so much more in her to give, and she wanted to give every drop of it to Jaxon. "Wow, stay-at-home mom." She couldn't resist stealing a kiss. "I can't believe we're really going to try this."

"You can go back to work anytime you want." He smiled. I can think of all sorts of jobs. Of course, there would be a rigorous interview process."

"Interview, huh?" She kissed him again. This time, she lingered and enjoyed the warmth of his mouth and the softness of his lips.

"Yes, but I could put in a good word or two." He ran a hand along the length of her back curving at her butt and then back to her shoulders before he kissed her again. "I love you."

"I love you, too, and I know I could go back to work at any time. It's just—I never thought this would happen for us." Years of wondering why her mother and father loved each other the way they did became as clear as if one of them had whispered some ancient secret into her ear. She understood why her mother dedicated her life to her husband and children, and why work had been a means to support them, not the purpose of her life. It hadn't made her mother weak to depend on her father. It'd made her family strong.

"And it makes you feel dependent on someone," he paused. "Does it scare you to depend on me?" His eyes held the question as much as his words.

"At first, I was petrified. But, I don't know. I can't explain. I'm not scared of being with you. I'm afraid to be without you. The only thing I can think about now is being the mother of your child and your wife." She kissed him again.

His arms tightened around her waist. "I'm so glad you came into my life. I can't wait until you become Mrs. Jaxon Slater."

"Hmmm. Have you ever thought about becoming Mr. Darling Crawford?" She laughed as she raked her fingers through his hair.

The strength of his embrace along with the gentle touch of his lips to hers dragged her heart deeper into his love. The deeper he kissed her, the more she knew she was never meant to be anywhere but where she was, in his arms and having his baby.

CHAPTER SIXTEEN

Darling popped the last slice of the juicy Clementine into her mouth and savored its sweet tanginess as she welcomed the warm breeze swirling around them. The quick wind whipped at her orange cotton sundress bellowing it slightly. Jaxon's hand disappeared in the folds of the fabric as he held it against her thigh. But, she welcomed its cooling flutter against her skin. And with the touch of his hand so close to the most delicate part of her, she needed that wind to cool and calm her.

It'd been too long since they'd had a day of doing nothing. The picnic Jaxon prepared included one of her new faves, smoked Gouda cheese. As she bit into another piece, she wondered why she'd never known it was so delicious!

Jaxon's hand rubbed the length of her rounded belly curving at the bottom before sliding back to the top. "Do you need anything to drink?"

Now that she was in the last weeks of her pregnancy, Jaxon had significantly cut back his time in the office to be with her. And she loved every moment. He'd spent too many long nights in the office in preparation for taking time off after the baby's birth. Soon, there would be three of them and she wanted just a little more time with nothing but the two of them. It was selfish, yes, but she didn't think she'd ever be able to love someone as much as she loved him. It might take time for her to get used to sharing him. No matter how much time they spent together, it was never enough. And when they made love, if it was possible, it was better than before the pregnancy. They had to get creative with her belly, but a few of their new tricks would definitely be used after the baby was born.

"No." She glanced over at her dwindling pile of cheese. "But, I think we're running low on Gouda." She arched her neck to look up at him with a smile.

He brushed a hand across her forehead, then let his fingers comb through her hair. "I didn't think you'd be able to finish that hunk of cheese by yourself."

"It's not me." She rubbed her belly. "It's your son. He demands cheese and oranges."

The smile that covered his face sent shivers through her. Little Jaxon kicked in response. She grabbed Jaxon's hand and positioned it, so he could feel the baby move, too.

At the first kick, his eyes widened.

Regardless of how many times they did this, she didn't think she'd ever tire of seeing his reaction. The only way to describe his response was love. Pure love for her and their son.

"You've made me happier than I ever thought I deserved to be. You know that right?" His other hand swiped at the bangs resting against her forehead.

"I feel the same." She sat up and leaned back into the hard wood planks of the park bench. "But, I—I still don't want this huge wedding." The day had been so wonderful and she didn't want to ruin it, but they'd been avoiding the conversation for weeks. "It gets bigger and bigger every day."

"Baby, I will give you a full-body massage every night for the rest of our lives." He smiled. "This wedding would make my mother so happy. She really wants to do this big 'wedding' thing." He waited. "She never thought this day would happen." He leaned over and kissed her, tenderly. "It would make her so happy."

She didn't want to be an ungrateful jerk, but she'd done the huge wedding thing before. Of course, her parents would love for her to have another big wedding in a church, too. But, she wasn't sure she wanted that this time. "The church part is fine, but…" She reached for her purse to retrieve the papers tucked inside.

"Wait, I'll get them," he said.

"Thank you." She flipped to the last page. "Babe, this list has hundreds of names on it. I don't recognize any of them, except for Annette and my parents."

He took the papers she offered and scanned them. "Do you want to invite anyone else?"

"No, babe, my point is I don't need anything this big." Her eyes fell to the huge stomach hiding her feet. "I just wanted it to be us and our families. Not all this."

"We could scale it back." He took a pen from her purse and began to cross out names. "I'll take care of it."

God, the look in his eyes broke her heart. He and his mother didn't want to do anything, but give her a big wedding, every woman's dream. And she knew her parents wanted this wedding because they hadn't been big fans of the first one. Her parents hadn't been allowed to be a part of Steve's planning of their wedding.

But, she'd had the big wedding and the marriage didn't last. This time, she wanted to make it smaller…just family. But, was the wedding the problem, or her dumb choice of the wrong man. Guilt shamed her, it wasn't fair of her. Jaxon hadn't been married. He deserved to have what she'd had, but she was a little afraid, maybe big weddings were bad luck.

Ridiculous. The sadness in his eyes cut through her fear. "I'm sorry, babe, whatever you want. I guess I'm a little scared about the big wedding thing."

"Why?" he asked.

"I did the whole big fancy wedding thing with Steve and what did that do for me?" She didn't want Jaxon to think she didn't want him. Sometimes, she still struggled with the shadows of her failed marriage.

He folded the pages in his hand and stuffed them back into her purse. Then, he swept her legs from the bench and placed them across his lap. Touching her chin, gently, he turned her face, so that her eyes met his. "That marriage is behind you." His lips touched hers. "I never thought I'd find a woman like you to share my life with. A woman I wanted to have a family with. And I want everyone I know to know that." With a hand on her stomach, he said, "I ran from this my entire life. But, I'm not running anymore. And I won't let you run."

"I don't deserve you." She traced her thumb over the shape of his lips. "I'm sorry that I keep screwing this up."

The smile that gave her a reason to wake early and go to bed late, just for a glance, sprung across his face. "Nothing you do would screw this up. And I promise, we'll scale back," he whispered through a kiss that sent shockwaves through her body awakening parts of her that only his touch could quiet.

Jaxon sat across the table from the bubbly wedding planner listening to their mothers bombard the poor woman with questions about every nuance of the wedding while Darling sampled cakes, quietly.

Whatever she'd tasted pleased her because she asked for another piece. "Here, honey, taste this," she said as she pushed a piece of something chocolaty into his mouth.

145

He made a mental note to buy the biggest thing of chocolate he could find as soon as possible. For the rest of his life, he wanted to lick chocolate from every part of her body. "I like it." It was good, but the frosting coating Darling's lips tempted him more. He leaned in and kissed her. "But, you taste better," he whispered against her lips. "How much longer do we have to be here?"

"Ask them." She pointed at their mothers who were so engaged they probably wouldn't have noticed if the two of them got up and walked out.

"I know I promised, but—" As much as he wanted to reel in their parents, he wanted them to go crazy. The woman sitting beside him made him proud. If she wanted, she could walk away from him, from everything and do whatever she set her mind on. He grew more thankful every day that that wasn't what she wanted.

Instead of sitting at home during the pregnancy, she'd decided to enroll in classes at Vanderbilt. Before their baby was two years old, she'd have her master's degree. When she went back to work for the company, she didn't want people whispering about her credentials. Hell, he had a master's too, but he only did it to get away from his father, not to be successful in business. He hadn't even wanted the damn company. But, now, he placed his hand on her stomach, it was about so much more than just him.

The forkful of cake she loaded into her mouth muddled her words. "It's...okay."

"No, I'll talk with them again. They've added names." As the list grew longer, he worried that she might back out. At one point, someone mentioned releasing butterflies. Butterflies!

"They're happy for us," she said.

He leaned in close and whispered against her ear, "Are you?" Damn, he didn't know what he'd do if she wasn't happy.

Her eyes closed briefly, and then they opened. "Yes."

The simple word rolled over him like warm molasses

calming the anxiousness he hadn't realized built as he waited for her response. But, no matter how much he wanted to accept it. He knew she was not happy with the extravagance of the wedding. "Mom, I think my future wife is getting tired. We're going to call it a day." He stood and reached for her hand to help her.

For the first time since they'd entered the shop, his mother and hers turned their attention away from the wedding planner and the pile of binders spread across the table in front of them. "But, son, we have so much more to do." She glanced at Mrs. Crawford for back up. "We haven't tasted half of these, yet." She pushed around some of the samples plated in front of them.

"You guys pick out what you like best. And we'll set-up another appointment later."

They kissed both women and left the small boutique bakery tucked away on one of Nashville's busiest streets. As the door closed, the delicious smells of raspberry and chocolate wafted out of shop behind them.

"So, what do you really want to do?" he asked as they strolled toward their car.

"Could we go for a walk?" she asked. "The sun feels wonderful on my skin."

"Were you cold inside?" He draped his arm over her shoulders.

"No. It's just that I think the baby likes the sun as much as I do." She placed a flat hand on her stomach. "He's kicking like mad." She smiled up at him.

He rested his hand on top of hers. "You're not tired?"

"No, not really and besides, the doctor said walking would be good for the baby. This has been the longest pregnancy ever!" She patted her stomach. "Maybe he'll come on out."

"He likes being inside of you." Jaxon smiled. "I know I do. Walking isn't the only activity the doctor recommended." He'd prefer his idea of activity to hers.

Darling snuggled into that spot underneath his arm that

had begun to feel empty when she wasn't there and wrapped her arms around his waist.

Walk it was.

CHAPTER SEVENTEEN

Only a handful of days remained before his son would be born. As Jaxon's taxi traveled the wide highways of Dallas, the soft jazz music piping from the taxi's radio didn't soothe his anger. The slow crawl of the taxi through Dallas' traffic pissed Jaxon off with each passing minute. He checked his watch again. Normally, he would welcome traveling to any of the offices to keep him away from whatever was happening in his life. But this time, it made him break his promise to one of the most important women in his life. If he missed his return flight, he would never be able to wash the taste of her tears on his lips from his nightmares. All morning, he'd tried to reassure her that he would return before the baby was born. Nothing he said stopped her tears.

Their baby could be born at any moment. His first-born son could come into the world without his father by his side. He'd lived most of his life without his father and now, he was about to curse his son's birth in the same way.

The carefully scripted speech from HR didn't mean a

damn thing to him as he burst into Rodney's office. "What in the hell are you doing?"

Rodney jumped from his office chair at the boom of the door against the wall behind it. "Sir?" he replied with a question.

The solid wood door thundered against its frame when Jaxon slammed it shut behind him. "Don't *sir* me. I sent you to Texas to avoid any problems between you and Barbara and now, you're doing the same bull here that you did in Memphis."

"Sir," Rodney said as he dropped into his chair. "I need my job."

"You don't act like it." The ignorant bastard didn't value anything and now, his actions affected Jaxon's family. He wanted to throw his ass out of a window. "What's wrong with you? You have a wife and kids," he paused. "Don't you care about them?"

"I missed her. I sent her a few pictures. I didn't think it would be a big deal."

"You didn't think it'd be a big deal to send naked pictures of yourself to the head of my Memphis division?" This guy was a damn idiot!

"No."

Did Rodney really believe the crap he was feeding to him, or was the guy such a big dumb ass that he thought he could still have a chance with a woman like Barbara? He'd had his doubts when Darling recommended her, but the woman had stepped up. She'd caught on quick, and reminded him and other doubters why she'd been hired in the first place. "What about the new employee here who filed harassment charges with HR?" Jaxon sifted through the emails on his phone in search of the employee's name. "Mary. Yes, Mary. What about her?"

Pink faced, Rodney responded, "Sir, my hand just brushed against her leg." He gulped down air. "I never meant anything by it and I immediately apologized."

"All three occasions were an accident? You think I'm a

fool?" There was a knock on the door. "Come in," Jaxon said.

Barbara entered flanked by security and his human resources manager.

"Rodney, I've given you too many chances. Barbara is going to run this office for a while until we determine who can manage things here for us."

Gloria, his human resources manager, stepped forward and handed Rodney a package.

"Rodney, I suggest you review and accept the package," Jaxon said.

"Sir, this isn't fair." The man's shoulders slumped. "I won't accept it. I—"

Is this idiot about to threaten me?

As much as he'd done for Rodney, was he about to jeopardize his ability to care for his family? He fisted both hands and with straight arms leaned forward on Rodney's desk. He gazed down into the man's eyes and wondered why he'd allowed this guy to risk the future of his company for so many years?

Because I didn't give a damn before now. But, now his son and the woman he would soon marry counted on it, on him, to take care of them. "Rodney, read it and sign. I've given you too many chances and now, I don't have time to deal with your shit anymore." He stepped back. "If you think you can challenge it, we can go down that road and I promise you won't be happy." He nodded at security. "They'll escort you out of the building." He glanced down at his watch and over at Barbara. "Barbara, you have my cell, I have to get back on a plane."

"I can handle it," she responded. "Say hi to your family for me."

Jaxon's phone rang with a special tone as he stepped into the waiting taxi. *Damn it!*

###

Darling swiped at the sweat matted hair laying over her face. "Mom, where is he?" she asked through gritted teeth as the pain rolling over her in waves slowly dulled to a tolerable level. "Where's the nurse?" She stared at the door. "Can't they give me something?"

"Not yet, honey." Her mother dabbed at her brow with a cool towel. "It's too early."

She bit down again, as another wave of pain hit her. "I can't believe he's not here." Tears sprang from her eyes, not because of the labor pains shooting through her, but because the man she loved—her baby's father, wasn't there beside her.

"Honey, he's on his way," her mother said.

As her mother set-up her comb and brush and began to tug at the wet tangled clumps of her hair, memories of years past when she and her sister would sit at her mother's feet waiting for their turn to have their mother plat and braid their hair washed over her. What kind of mother would she be? What kind of parents would she and Jaxon be together?

"He promised." Tears fell hard and fast. They would be horrible parents. He wasn't with her, they weren't married and she'd already failed at marriage and as a wife before. "It was more important for him to be in Texas than here with me."

"No, baby, it wasn't," his mother said rubbing a comforting hand down her arm.

"Then why isn't he here?" She wanted to scream it, but she didn't.

"We called him baby, he'll be here before you know it," her mother soothed.

"He said he loved me. He said he wanted to have a family and get married, but when he had to choose between his family and his work, he chose it over us." This time the contraction that hit her raised her body from the bed, and she didn't hold back the scream building inside of her.

Both her mother and Mrs. Slater were caressing her face and arms with cool wet towels before the scream finished. Softly, they wiped away the sweat that had beaded on her skin.

Her father stood from his seated position in a nearby corner. "No, Darling, he didn't choose his work over you. He's protecting his business, so he can provide for you and his new family. That's what we want to do as men…take care of our families." Her father leaned down and kissed her sweaty forehead. "I would've done it, too." He pointed to the women in the room. "He knew you had family who would be here with you until he arrived. I know he'll be here, soon."

She listened to her father, but even with them beside her, it didn't feel complete without Jaxon. And she believed in her heart the baby knew he wasn't there, too. He was as angry as she was. "Dad, how am I supposed to agree with that when I'm here by myself…again?"

"No, sweetie, you're not alone. You have us," he repeated. "You'll never be alone again."

Her doctor entered the room.

"How are we doing in here?" The doctor scanned the sad faces and hurried to her bedside. "Is everything okay?" She placed a hand on her stomach and with the most gentle touch applied pressure in a few places on her belly.

"Yes," the response came from everyone.

Before responding, her doctor applied more pressure and briefly listened to the rhythm of her breathing. "Great. Who's going to stay in the room while I take a quick look?"

Her father left.

"Okay, well let's see what's going on." The doctor's head disappeared, briefly. "Well, it looks like it's time," she proclaimed with a big smile.

"My baby," her mother said with tears in her eyes. The women hugged each other with tears rolling down their cheeks.

Darling wanted to cry, too, but not for the same reasons. Jaxon had promised to be with her.

Jaxon's mother flipped open her phone and stepped out into the hallway.

With his suit jacket gripped in a sweaty fist, Jaxon raced through the halls of the hospital, searching. He stripped the damn tie that kept flapping in his face from his neck and shoved it into one of his pockets. Turn after turn, he went the wrong direction. Why was he so damn lost? He'd been to the hospital before. Their doctor had offices in the building and they'd prepared for the baby's birth too many times for him to be confused now.

He paused at an elevator and dialed his mother's number again.

"Sir, can I help you?" a nurse asked with concern.

He stuffed the phone back in his pocket. "Yes, I'm trying to find my wi—Darling. Darling Crawford."

"Oh, yes, sir, they are in her room." The nurse smiled.

Jaxon didn't want to think through what the nurse said. But, there was no way to deny what she'd implied. "They are in her room? I was told she was here."

"Yes, sir, she was. The delivery was an easy one." She smiled warmly. "She's in her room with the baby." She pointed at elevators further down the hallway. "Downstairs, one floor. They'll be able to help you."

The gravity of the nurse's words punched Jaxon in his heart. He'd missed the birth of his first child. His son. He'd broken his promise. The elevator dinged at him, but he barely noticed.

"Sir, are you going down?" a young woman asked, while patiently holding the elevator.

"Yes, I'm sorry." He entered the elevator. "Thank you." The ride down ended in an instant, but he could barely make his feet move.

When he crossed the elevator's threshold, Jaxon ran. But, his feet wouldn't carry him fast enough. The beat of his heart grew louder in his ears the faster he ran. What would he do if she didn't forgive him for being an idiot and missing their son's birth? What would he do if she walked out of his life forever?

At the door, he stood and listened to the coos and words of love spoken by his loved ones on the other side of the door. He raked a nervous hand through his hair. Only one choice could be made, but damn the door to her room weighed more than he lifted in the gym.

The voices quieted when he entered. All eyes focused on him, except the ones that mattered most...Darling's gaze didn't turn away from the bundle in her arms.

His mother approached him first and kissed him on the cheek. "Son, he's beautiful." She wiped away tears streaming from her eyes. "He looks just like you did when you were born."

"Son," her father said, "we'll give you guys a few minutes alone." He rounded up the two women and left. But, not before Mrs. Crawford kissed the same cheek his mother had.

He wanted to run to her bedside, but again he was frozen where he stood. He'd give anything to be in a boardroom where he knew what to do. Here he was lost. Only a few feet away, his son rested on the breast of the woman he loved, but he didn't think she wanted him near either of them.

"You don't have to be here," she said without glancing away from their sleeping son. She rested her chin against his forehead and closed her eyes.

Jaxon didn't know the name of the tune she hummed, but their son wriggled in her arms in response to the music.

If he didn't take charge, now, he might actually lose her because he didn't deserve her forgiveness. "Baby." He walked to her bedside. "I promise it will never happen again." He didn't think he could bare it if she didn't look at him. He needed her to see him. To believe him when he said he'd never hurt her or their son again.

"Of course not. It would be a miracle for me to have another child." Tears began to fall. "I needed you." She kissed their son. Finally, she looked at him, but he wasn't prepared for the sadness in her eyes. "I needed you—we needed you." She tightened her hold on their son who was now silently resting in her arms.

"I know." What else could he say? "I could've let HR manage Rodney, but I wanted to be there. I wanted him to know that there were no more second chances." He moved closer still. "I never cared much about the company. I blamed it on my father leaving my mother." His thoughts raced as he tried to focus. "I'd turned my back on it and allowed others in the company to take control. Rodney was one of those people. And he abused his power and my trust." He reached out and ran a finger across his son's cheek. The instant he touched his son, he knew he could never be like his father. He could never walk away from either of them. Whatever it took to get her forgiveness, he would do it. "I have too much to lose now. I have a family to take care of."

"If you can't put us first now, will you be able to ever?" She planted small kisses all over their son's face. "You'll never get to see his birth. You missed it. What else will you miss?" Tears streamed down her face. "You promised me," she cried.

"Nothing. I promise. I won't miss anything. No birthdays. No anniversaries. Nothing."

Even his own father had been at his birth. What kind of man misses the birth of his first child? He couldn't remember the last time he'd cried, but at the crisp clear sound of his son's cries, he shed his own tears.

The anger in Darling's eyes softened as his tears fell. She watched as he stood there wiping away the sign of his own pain.

"Darling, I love you and my son." He tugged at the blankets covering Jaxon Jr. and knew he had to give her the choice. "Do you want me to leave? I want to be here." He stared into the eyes of the woman who'd just given birth to his son and something happened to his heart. He knew that even if she told him to get the hell out, he would keep coming back until she put a restraining order against him. There was no way he could actually leave them.

Her silence killed him.

His heart grew heavier as he stepped away from them and decided he should at least go to the waiting room outside and talk with their parents. Maybe, he could get them to talk to her for him.

Jaxon took another step back.

Darling reached for his hand. "Do you want to hold him?"

He reached for his son, and as they shifted him from her arms to his, his son's hiccupped cries quieted.

She smiled, weakly. "He knows you're his dad."

The bronzed skin of his son was a perfect blend of theirs. He traced a finger over their baby's chin and his cries stopped. "You think so." He dared to take another look into her eyes. Each time he did, he would swear she stole another piece of him.

She ran her fingers through her hair loosening tangles as she reached the ends. She continued the process until she was satisfied. Since the pregnancy, she'd decided to let her hair grow. After smoothing it, she twisted her hair into a bun and knotted it on top of her head.

With no make-up and untamed hair, she was still the most beautiful woman he knew.

"You made him stop crying." She smiled.

"How is it possible to love someone so completely, so quickly?" He sat in the chair beside the bed holding his son with his baby's mother watching. *Baby's mama.* That had to change... he needed to marry her quick. "He feels so fragile." He held him tighter and kissed his cheek. "I can't believe I missed his birth."

"You can make it up to us." Darling elevated her bed and reached for him. Pulling him by his shirt, she closed the distance between them. "I love you Jaxon Slater. I'm mad as hell that you weren't here." She cupped his face between her hands. "I was so afraid."

"I know." He leaned closer and kissed her. "What do I have to do to make it up to you?"

A beautiful sexy grin he'd never seen before crossed her face. "Lots and lots of things."

Hours later, Jaxon's feet dangled from a cot the staff had rolled into Darling's room. He'd missed the birth and he couldn't take that back, but he refused to leave the hospital until they did. They'd taken Jaxon Jr. back to the hospital nursery. Unable to sleep, he rested on the creaky cot staring out of the hospital room window. The full moon that stared back at him mocked him for his inability to be the man he needed to be. Would he be a role model for his son? One day, his son would need his birth certificate for something, and it would show his first mistake—too afraid to marry the woman he loved, the way she wanted him to marry her.

Darling woke to sounds of chaos around her. Her parents and Jaxon's mother were moving around the room with such purpose, she couldn't figure out what they were doing. Squinting at the bright sunlight pooling through the windows of her private room, she tried to orient herself. The dull burning sensation that quickly spread through her lower body reminded her of where she was and what had happened. She'd given birth to her son, Jaxon. And even though he was late, his father hadn't left her alone. Instead, he'd spent the entire night on a rollaway bed barely big enough for her.

She turned toward the other bed to say good morning.

But, he wasn't there. "Mom, what's going on?" She searched the room for Jaxon and the baby. "Is it feeding time? Where is Jaxon?"

"Jaxon will be back shortly." Her mom smiled at her over her shoulder. "We're getting ready."

"For what?" She tugged at the short thin blankets on her bed. But, she felt no warmer.

"A wedding," Jaxon's mother answered with a bigger smile.

Where these two ladies losing it? Who has a wedding in a hospital? "A wedding?" She puffed up the pillows behind her and slid up a little in bed. "Who? What?" Where was Jaxon?

Her mom opened a box and held up a beautiful white wedding dress. "Jaxon picked it out." Using one of her arms, her mother fluffed out the white fabric for Darling's approval.

The empire cut dress was as long as her mother was tall, which meant it would drag the floor on her. "My wedding!" She reached for the dress. It was simple with no beading, just beautiful chiffon. And it would be forgiving of her belly. "It's beautiful," she cried.

"He spent all morning picking out the perfect dress," his mother said.

"'Bout time," her father added.

Darling combed her fingers through her hair, and then dragged them over her face. "But, my hair and make-up." He may accept her just as she was, and she may be having a wedding in a hospital, but that didn't mean she had to look like she'd been dug up by the cat.

"We've got that covered," his mother said.

Both women flashed huge smiles. "Your mom and I are at your service," Jaxon's mother replied as both women wrapped their arms around each other. "We're your personal stylists today."

"So, let's get you up and into the shower," her mom added.

She didn't want their parents to be upset or feel they'd missed out on anything because they weren't having the big wedding with all the crazy trimmings. "Mom, Mrs. Slater, I know you guys had big plans."

They looked at each other. "We did. But, this is your wedding," her mother replied. "You should have the wedding you want."

"Besides, we can still have a big party. Right?" his mom asked.

"Yes, ma'am. We can definitely have a party." She smiled. "A huge one!"

As she headed toward the shower, another thought hit her. "Mom, what about shoes?"

Her mom opened another box. "What do you think?" She held up a beautiful pair of flat white ballet slippers.

Perfect for a woman who just had a baby and didn't want to wear heels. "Love them!"

With a little help from her mom and Mrs. Slater, she disappeared into the shower.

Inside the hospital chapel surrounded by her doctor and the nurses who'd assisted with the birth of their son, she and the man she loved faced the hospital's pastor. Everyone, including Jaxon, wanted her to sit in a wheelchair, but that wasn't going to happen. Her legs were a little wobbly, but it didn't matter. Her doctor and every nurse marveled at how quickly she was recuperating for a first pregnancy. And she felt like she could do anything. So, no, she would stand at Jaxon's side.

"I can't believe you guys pulled this together while I slept," she said to Jaxon as they stood in front of the hospital's pastor.

"Believe it," Jaxon responded with a smile that she would never grow tired of seeing.

"What? Were you afraid I would run?"

"Yes," he whispered. "And I've waited long enough to make you my wife." His arms wrapped around her waist, pulling her tight to his body.

The first touch of his lips to hers buckled her knees. Only the strength of his arms around her held her upright.

The pastor cleared his throat. "It's not quite time for that, yet." He smiled.

"Sorry, sir. Just practicing," Jaxon said as he released her.

Jaxon Jr. whaled at the sound of his father's voice.

"Looks like we'd better hurry this up. Someone's hungry," Darling added.

Jaxon quirked an eyebrow at her. Heat burst through her body. It took nothing for Jaxon to melt her. Even though she'd just given birth, the only thing she could think about was when she would be able to feel his mouth, his hands, all of him again.

The next weeks would be hard, but as the pastor began the ceremony, joy filled her at the thought of spending the rest of her life with her husband and their beautiful baby boy.

The following is an excerpt from *Love's Chance* by Angela Kay Austin.

Sinclair emerged from the bathroom. "I'm ready." Golden dreadlocks crinkled into big twists cascaded down around her shoulders. Although not revealing, her tangerine blouse hugged her full bosom, then lay over the top of the waistband of her jeans. Jeans that hugged the curves of her hips and thighs.

DAMN. Immediately, his body reacted to hers. It took Chance a moment to rise from his chair.

"I'm ready," Sinclair repeated.

"Okay, so what do you want to do first? Casino downstairs or maybe walk under the lights on Freeman?"

Her eyes twinkled as she answered, "Lights."

"Okay, lights it is. Let's go grab a taxi."

The cab ride to Freeman Street felt like the longest ride of his life. With her eyes closed, she rested her head on his shoulder the entire trip. Each rub of her cheek against his shoulder matched the caress of her breasts against his arm as she found the right spot to doze. Touch after touch increased his ache. His need and desire. His khaki pants pulled tighter against his body with each meeting of their bodies. Before the taxi dropped them at their destination, he hoped he could regain control.

When the taxi pulled up to the curb, he grew anxious, but he had to wake her in order to reach his wallet. After paying the driver and quickly counting to ten, he opened the door and they hopped out. "Sinclair you seem really tired. Maybe we should head back."

"No, I'll be fine." She yawned and stretched.

Chance draped his arm around her and they walked. "Okay, Cinderella, we'll have you home before midnight."

"So, if I'm Cinderella, are you my Prince Charming?"

"Maybe not Prince Charming, but the Frog Prince."

"Hmm…Frog Prince. So, I have to kiss you to break the curse?"

Chance stopped. He slowly backed Sinclair up against a brick wall and stared at her lips. He wanted to kiss her. For about six months, he'd wanted to. "You have to kiss me to break the spell. That's true."

Her breathing sped up to match his. "What spell?"

He couldn't play the game any longer. "Sinclair, will you stop me?"

"Stop you? Chance, I—" Her words halted.

Chance's hands explored Sinclair's body. Slowly, he dragged them up and down along her butt, thighs and back. He placed his hands on either side of her head and intertwined his fingers in her locks. "Sinclair. Yes or no."

"Ye—"

Chance didn't wait for her to finish. Her mouth opened to his. The warmth of her tongue increased his desire. This time, he didn't count to ten or hide it. He pressed his body to hers and hers against the stone behind her.

Petite hands grabbed at the back of his shirt, pulling him closer.

ABOUT THE AUTHOR

Angela Kay Austin has always loved expressing herself creatively. An infatuation with music led to years playing several instruments, some better than others. A love for acting put her in front of a camera or two for her thirty seconds of fame before giving way to a degree and career in communications. After completing a second degree in marketing, Angela found herself combining her love for all things creative and worked in promotions and events for many years.

Today, Angela lives in her hometown in Tennessee with her really, really, really old dog, Midnight.

To learn more about Angela, visit her website:
AngelaKayAustin.com

- Started in theater.

- Self published

- Why Memphis

who are
you
inspiration
Writer

Barbara
$
Darling relationship

- Beverley Jenkins
A first romance
writer

Made in the USA
Monee, IL
06 June 2020